He wasn't supposed to be here. Not in the diner. This was her part of town!

"Brie?"

In her fantasies, they met one day in Salem or Boston or some other big city where she was a respected businesswoman. She would, of course, be perfectly dressed and not at all troubled by the sight of the only man she had ever loved. In reality, she couldn't utter a word.

"What are you doing here?" he asked.

His incredulous expression made it a whole lot easier to swallow the emotions churning inside her. She sensed his pity, and that steadied her. Conscious of the roomful of people, she settled for a terse reply.

"I work here. What are you doing? Out slumming?"

Again fluttered unspoken in the heavy air.

His eyes narrowed. She couldn't help but notice his thick black lashes, tipped with gold—just like their daughter's.

Dear Harlequin Intrigue Reader,

We've got another explosive lineup of four thrilling titles for you this month. Like you'd expect anything less of Harlequin Intrigue—*the* line for breathtaking romantic suspense.

Sylvie Kurtz returns to east Texas in *Red Thunder Reckoning* to conclude her emotional story of the Makepeace brothers in her two-book FLESH AND BLOOD series. Dani Sinclair takes *Scarlet Vows* in the third title of our modern Gothic continuity, MORIAH'S LANDING. Next month you can catch Joanna Wayne's exciting series resolution in *Behind the Veil*.

The agents at Debra Webb's COLBY AGENCY are taking appointments this month—fortunately for one woman who's in serious jeopardy. But with a heartthrob Latino bodyguard for protection, it's uncertain who poses the most danger—the killer *or* her *Personal Protector*.

Finally, in a truly innovative story, Rita Herron brings us to NIGHTHAWK ISLAND. When one woman's hearing is restored by an experimental surgery, she's awakened to the sound of murder in *Silent Surrender*. But only one hardened detective believes her. And only he can guard her from certain death.

So don't forget to pick up all four for a complete reading experience. Enjoy!

Sincerely,

Denise O'Sullivan
Associate Senior Editor
Harlequin Intrigue

SCARLET VOWS
DANI SINCLAIR

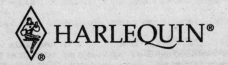

TORONTO • NEW YORK • LONDON
AMSTERDAM • PARIS • SYDNEY • HAMBURG
STOCKHOLM • ATHENS • TOKYO • MILAN • MADRID
PRAGUE • WARSAW • BUDAPEST • AUCKLAND

Special thanks and acknowledgment
are given to Dani Sinclair for her contribution
to the MORIAH'S LANDING series.

ISBN 0-373-22658-6

SCARLET VOWS

Visit us at www.eHarlequin.com

Printed in U.S.A.

ABOUT THE AUTHOR

An avid reader, Dani Sinclair didn't discover romance novels until her mother lent her one when she'd come for a visit. Dani's been hooked on the genre ever since. But she didn't take up writing seriously until her two sons were grown. Since the premiere of *Mystery Baby* for Harlequin Intrigue in 1996, Dani's kept her computer busy. Her third novel, *Better Watch Out,* was a RITA® Award finalist in 1998. Dani lives outside Washington, D.C., a place she's found to be a great source for both intrigue and humor!

You can write to her in care of the Harlequin Reader Service.

Books by Dani Sinclair

HARLEQUIN INTRIGUE
371—MYSTERY BABY
401—MAN WITHOUT A BADGE
448—BETTER WATCH OUT
481—MARRIED IN HASTE
507—THE MAN SHE MARRIED
539—FOR HIS DAUGHTER*
551—MY BABY, MY LOVE*
565—THE SILENT WITNESS*
589—THE SPECIALIST
602—BEST-KEPT SECRETS*
613—SOMEONE'S BABY
658—SCARLET VOWS

*Fools Point/Mystery Junction

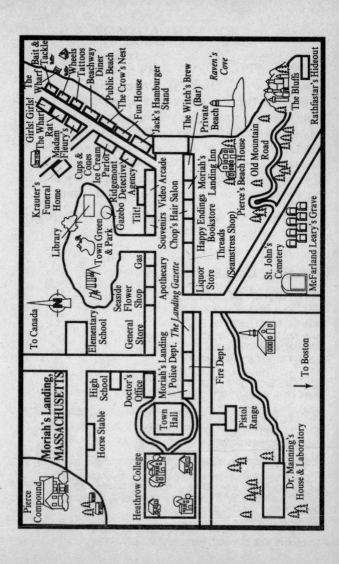

CAST OF CHARACTERS

Andrew "Drew" Pierce—He had no idea his decision to run for mayor would have so many consequences.

Brianna "Brie" Dudley—Her daughter's no secret, but the father is.

Nancy Bell—She planned to be more than Drew's publicist.

Dr. David Bryson—Drew blames the reclusive scientist for the death of his sister.

Claire Cavendish—Has the person who kidnapped and tortured her five years ago returned?

Nicole Dudley—Brianna's three-year-old daughter truly is a little witch.

Carey Eldrich—Drew's best friend and fiercest competitor loves women, but did he love one to death?

McFarland Leary—He may be dead, but he's far from forgotten.

Dr. Leland Manning—The geneticist is called a vampire behind his back.

Ursula Manning—Leland's much younger wife set everything in motion with her shocking death.

Geoffrey Pierce—Drew's uncle feels unappreciated by his peers, but he plans to change all that with his secretive research.

Edgar "Razz" Razmuesson—Razz and his friend Dodie are probably behind a lot of the mischief in Moriah's Landing, but how far is he willing to go for money and a little revenge?

Frederick Thane—Is the current mayor intending to keep his position at any cost?

My thanks to Priscilla Berthiaume for the concept; to Denise O'Sullivan for allowing me to participate; to my fellow writers for their efforts to make it all gel; to Officers Kelly Flannigan, Melissa Parlon and Gary Sommers, whose information and instruction were terrific; to Susan King and Mary McGowan for their support; and a special, GREAT BIG THANKS to Josh King, whose time and information was invaluable. Any errors are mine alone.

And as always, for Roger, Chip, Dan and Barb. Love you!

Prologue

Eerie stillness blanketed the morning air over Moriah's Landing. The troubled town brooded beneath the sweltering heat, expectantly waiting.

Her customers all served for the moment, Brianna Dudley pushed at the damp tendril of hair clinging to her forehead and wiped her hands on her apron. Even in the air-conditioned diner it was too hot. A sense of something about to happen crawled over her skin.

Brie stepped outside, moving across the newly attached deck at the back of the Beachway Diner.

Waves lapped steadily at the public beach stretched out below. She checked the deserted tables around her automatically before looking toward the undefined horizon. Definitely too hot for this early in the morning. A scan of the horizon failed to reveal any gathering clouds. She'd hoped that might account for the unease whispering over her nerve endings. Storms always made her tense.

A lazy gull swooped over the restless cove in search of food. He swept past the lighthouse before soaring toward the cliffs and the old stone castle that perched there.

Truly eerie and somber, the forbidding stone fortress

would have done justice to the cover of a gothic novel. Clinging precariously to the edge of a jagged cliff, the Bluffs even came equipped with a dark, brooding scientist. Rumor had it Dr. David Bryson was a cold-blooded murderer, horribly disfigured in the explosion that had taken his fiancée's life.

Brie didn't know David all that well, but his fiancée, Tasha Pierce, had been one of her best friends, and she truly believed he'd loved Tasha. David was seldom seen in town, but it didn't seem to occur to people that rather than being a recluse, perhaps he worked all day. And if he shunned bright lights, Brie understood. He had been scarred when his boat exploded in a wild ball of flame.

People here, especially the fishermen, tended toward the superstitious. The older ones loved to spin a good yarn and David Bryson was a terrific target, especially now that Moriah's Landing was bent on capitalizing on the wickedness that haunted their past. Salem held the historical reputation, but the founders of Moriah's Landing had joined the fanaticism of the time, punishing helpless men and women for the art of witchcraft.

Whatever secrets the castle on the cliffs held or didn't hold, it overlooked the cove in sinister silence. No one denied that dark forces seemed to emanate from those old stone walls.

Brie turned away from the sight. Shortly, she would be too busy to worry about castles, witches, the weather or anything else. The annual shooting tournament at the firing range was tomorrow. The event would kick off the weeklong Fourth of July festivities. Since the town was celebrating its three-hundred-and-fiftieth year, they were going all out, trying to surpass the spectacular Memorial Day weekend blast. The scheduled activities had raised the town spirits high. Moriah's Landing and the surrounding areas were filling with visitors and summer vacationers who thought flocking to the Massachusetts coast would provide some relief from the heat wave sweeping the country. Ha! Not even a puff of wind stirred the terrible humidity.

Brie planned to go over to the firing range before work tomorrow. With luck she could catch her mother's doctor, Sheffield Thornton, while her mother wasn't around. She wanted a flat answer to the question gnawing a hole in her soul.

Inside, the air conditioner continued its desperate struggle against Mother Nature. Brie inhaled the chilled air gratefully. Yvette Castor raised a summoning hand from her solitary seat in a booth near the window. Her many-ringed fingers waggled, the multitude of bracelets clanging merrily as she motioned for her check.

"Anything else, Yvette? More coffee?"

"No, thanks. I have to get over to my shop. Cassandra has the day off and I'm doing an early-morning reading for one of my regulars."

The floor-length broom skirt was cinched at her waist by several lengths of silver and gold chains. Like the bangles adorning her arms and neck, they jingled noisily each time she moved. Yvette had become a part of the local color in more ways than one. Today's bold purple peasant blouse clashed cheerfully with most of the colors in her skirt. Yvette wasn't a pretty woman, with that square jaw and those sharply defined features, but she was arresting. Her untamable mass of frizzy dark brown curls tumbled wildly down her back, nearly to her waist. Yet there was a down-to-earth quality about Yvette that Brie liked and respected.

Running Madam Fleury's fortune-telling stand across the street from the diner suited Yvette. At times there was an almost mystical quality about the woman. Brie couldn't imagine her doing anything else.

"How is your mother today, Brianna?"

The reminder of her mother's drawn features this morning made Brie grimace. "The heat's getting to her."

More than the heat, and both women knew it. There was no way Brie could pretend any longer that the cancerous tumor hadn't returned. After the last attempt to remove it, Dr. Thornton warned if the tumor began to grow again, it would only be a matter of time.

Brie swallowed hard against the knot at the back of her throat. Her hand quivered as she handed Yvette her check. Their fingers collided. A warm tingle spread like waves of invisible energy right up Brie's arm from that point of contact. For a timeless second, everything seemed to stop. Yvette seemed to gaze straight inside her soul.

Brie yanked her hand back. Yvette grasped the check before it could flutter to the tabletop. Her gaze never wavered.

"Do not worry," Yvette said quietly. "Closure is at hand."

A stab of genuine fear made Brie inhale sharply.

"No! I'm sorry, Brianna. I phrased my words poorly. I didn't mean your mother." She offered an apologetic smile. "I should have said 'Your prince is coming.'"

Brie didn't know whether to laugh or scold Yvette for the moment of intense fear her words had caused. Relief won. Yet something in that mesmerizing gaze made it hard to doubt her quietly spoken words. Brie forced her fingers to ease their death grip on her pad. She tossed her hair back, giving her head a negative shake.

"Now, what on earth would I want with a prince?" she demanded. "I already have enough people to serve." Brie indicated the diner at large, beginning to fill with the usual morning crowd. "And I'd better get back to work before I get fired."

"Brianna."

A warning prickle scaled its way down her spine. Unable to leave, but not wanting to hear any more talk about princes, or discuss her mother's illness, Brianna tried to force her legs to take the necessary steps away from the table. She couldn't.

"Things happen for a reason, you know," Yvette said softly. "You must learn to trust your heart once more."

For a moment, his features were right there in her mind, as vivid and alive as the man himself. Brie could almost see the way the sun placed golden highlights in his hair. She could almost smell the scent of the ridiculously expensive aftershave he wore. And without even closing her eyes, she felt the power of his body as he drew her into the embrace she had craved for what seemed like eternity.

"No!"

Brie lowered her voice quickly. No one spared her a glance. She tried for a smile but was only partially successful. "Forget it, Yvette. I made the mistake of trusting my heart once before. It didn't work out."

Yvette gazed right through her pretense. "Was it really a mistake?"

Jolted, Brie mustered a glare. Everyone knew Brie's young daughter, Nicole, was the joy of her life. While definitely an unplanned pregnancy, her daughter's birth was a gift. Nicole was growing into a miniature version of both Brie and her mother. The three of them could have been clones, down to the unfortunate bright red hair, pale skin and light freckles sprinkled liberally across cheeks and noses.

Everything except their eyes.

While Brie and her mother's eyes sparkled a clear, bewitching green, Nicole's were a startlingly vivid, brilliant blue shade. Piercing. Expressive eyes. Old eyes, her mother had once mused. Brie didn't know about that, but she did know that her daughter's eyes were a constant, uncomfortable reminder of the incredibly sexy man who had fathered her.

"So maybe it wasn't a total mistake," she conceded, not wanting to think about Andrew Pierce. But her foolish, stupid heart gave its usual lurch at the memories she had never learned to suppress. "But falling in love is a mistake I won't ever make again."

"Perhaps that was not a mistake, either, just mistimed."

Brie suppressed a bitter laugh. "Oh it was mistimed, all right. Take it from me, Yvette, I learned one important fact the summer Nicole was conceived. Princes have a disturbing habit of turning into frogs."

She tore her gaze from the sympathy and understanding in Yvette's sad expression, acutely grateful for the gruff, burly biker who indicated he and his companion were ready to place their order.

"I'll be right with you, Rider," she called out. To Yvette she added lightly, "Thanks just the same, but I'll pass on any more princes. I don't have time for fairy tales anymore."

Or the Pierce family—Andrew Pierce in particular.

"Fairy tales can come true," Yvette said softly.

"Ha! Mine would need a fairy godmother with the

cure for cancer. If you meet any, feel free to send them my way. Have a good day, Yvette."

Brie moved briskly to where the two scruffy-looking bikers waited with stoic patience.

Andrew Pierce was undoubtedly some woman's idea of a prince, she thought, but not hers. Not anymore.

WITH HER SCREAM reverberating in his ears, he watched in detachment as her delicate features twisted in comprehension and horror.

"Ursula."

He said her name sharply, reaching for her. She scuttled away with surprising speed. How unfortunate. She was going to make him do this the hard way. The bloodied gloves made getting a good grip on her all but impossible. Terror gave her a strength she wouldn't normally have.

He peeled the gloves from his hands. They dropped to the floor with a wet plopping sound.

"Ursula, stop this."

"My God! My God!"

Fists pressed against parted lips, her eyes wide, dark pools of horror. Her gaze seemed mesmerized by the still figure on the table, bathed in the bright surgical lights. He had peeled back the skull to reveal the all important brain.

"You killed her!"

"Calm down."

The hand pressing against her mouth trembled violently. "You killed her!"

She backed into a lab table deep in the shadows of the room. Objects clattered in protest. A pair of test tubes fell together with a jarring crash. He took a step closer. Frantically, her hand swept the table in search of a weapon.

She really was quite beautiful, he decided in detachment. Beautiful, sensual—immoral. Yet even in her panic there was a delicate grace about her.

"This is unfortunate. You shouldn't have come in here," he told her regretfully.

A test tube hurled toward his face. He turned his head and the empty vial bounced off his shoulder, falling harmlessly to the floor. She twisted, turning to run. His lips curved. Grotesque shadows danced about the lab, thrown by those bright lights over the exam table where the nude body lay still as marble.

"You're being foolish, my dear. There's nowhere for you to run, you know."

Her panicked breathing made harsh, raspy sounds as she scrambled around a bank of storage cases, nearly falling. He'd planned to confront her later, after he'd finished his work. What had made her decide to come in here now? Not that it mattered. The results would have been the same either way.

His footfalls were the only other sound in the room as he stalked her, cutting off each avenue of escape. She was lost. Confused by the darkness. When she fled between a tall storage cabinet and the untidy stack of large pine boxes, he had her. She'd chosen a dead end in the maze of disorganized equipment.

"Stay away from me! Don't come near me!"

"Poor Ursula."

"Let me go!"

"You know I can't do that. Not now. It's too bad, really. I'd hoped this would work out much differently."

She screamed, the shrill sound hurting his ears. Even

in the darkness he could see that her eyes were so wide with fear they dominated her small face. His pity was cold comfort for both of them.

"Poor, traitorous Ursula. You really shouldn't have come in here," he said sadly, pinning her flailing arms in a grip she had no chance of breaking. "You've left me no choice. None at all."

Chapter One

Andrew "Drew" Pierce gazed around at the large crowd gathered outside the firing range in frustration. "Where's Carey?"

"He had to see a man about a horse," Zach announced.

At the same time, Nancy Bell replied, "He went to use the men's room."

Drew gave the attractive brunette an apologetic look before scolding his much younger brother with a frown of reprimand. Zach shrugged, but his grin was unrepentant.

"That was his expression, not mine," Zach said. "How much do you two have riding on this bet? They're always competing with each other," he said in an aside to Nancy. "I think you scared the—"

"There is no bet," Drew said sharply. "And watch your language, Zach."

"It's all right, Andrew," Nancy told him, her soft, graceful hand a stark contrast against his tanned arm. "I could probably even teach Zach a few phrases."

Drew rolled his eyes. "Please don't."

"Think so?" Zach inquired with a broad smile that revealed two hidden dimples.

"You'd be amazed at what I deal with in my line of work."

"Maybe so, but you don't have to deal with it from Zach," Drew warned.

Zach held up his palms. "Sorry, big brother, for a moment there I forgot about your image."

Drew's frown deepened. There was an edge to his brother's tone and a strange undercurrent of emotion beneath the impish expression. Drew turned away thoughtfully. He sensed, rather than saw, Zach lean toward Nancy. Sotto voce, Zach asked, "Like what, for example?"

Drew never heard her response. The tournament had brought out a large crowd as always, and there was a festive air despite the heat. People milled in scattered clumps, chatting and laughing loudly as they waited for their turn to compete. The scent of grilled hot dogs and fresh popcorn mingled bizarrely with the scent of cordite in the heavy air.

A disturbing sensation pulled Drew's attention to the thick clump of trees that began halfway up the slope on one side of the pistol range. He stared at the dark line of woods, puzzled. Something had changed a short way into the tree line, but he wasn't sure what that something was.

Deer?

The woods were filled with the animals, but no deer would be within twenty miles of the noise coming from the firing range. Nancy and Zach added laughter to the din. Drew tuned them out. His attention centered on the shadows up the slope. Without knowing why, he concentrated on a dark patch near a wide maple tree. Beads of sweat collected at his hairline and trickled warmly down his back beneath his light summer shirt.

Nothing moved in the patch of trees, yet Drew sensed a presence there. Someone was watching him.

His fingers tightened on the gun case. He had a strange impulse to pull his weapon and aim it toward that spot on the hill.

As if sensing that thought, the darkness stirred.

The motion was slight, hardly a movement at all, but Drew waited, rigid with expectation. A face suddenly appeared, for all the world looking like a disembodied head floating in midair.

Eyes clashed and held.

Drew swore viciously under his breath. The features were unmistakable.

Zach broke off midsentence, coming alert. "What's the matter?"

"Andrew?" Nancy asked in concern.

"Bryson," he growled.

The face melted back into the shadows as if it had never been there at all.

"David Bryson?" Zach demanded. "Where?"

"Who's David Bryson?" Nancy questioned.

"In the trees up the hill," Drew told his brother with a small nod.

"I don't see anything."

Nancy squeezed his arm in a bid for attention. "Andrew? Who is David Bryson?"

In that brief moment of eye contact with the man, rage had surged inside Drew, welling from the recesses where he kept it mostly caged. Now he worked to contain a whole host of emotions, feeling his jaw clench. His knuckles whitened on the case in his hand. He looked at Nancy without really seeing her.

"David Bryson is the bastard who killed our sister."

"*What?*"

"I still don't see anyone," Zach said, watching the trees with the same tense wariness Drew had felt only moments earlier.

"He's gone now," Drew told him with certainty. "Back to the shadows where he belongs."

"I thought your sister's death was an accident," Nancy said sharply.

"That's how they classified it," Zach agreed, equally grim.

Drew didn't believe those findings. He never had. Their beautiful sister, Tasha, would have been alive today if it hadn't been for David Bryson. One day, Drew would prove he'd been responsible for what happened. In the meantime, he'd concentrate on winning the mayoral election. Then he'd be in a position to make Dr. David Bryson wish he'd died in that boat explosion as well.

"Oh, hell," Zach said, abruptly. "Just what we need. More trouble. Ten o'clock high."

Frederick Thane was working the crowd, moving in their direction. The current mayor stopped abruptly, his double chin quivering when he spotted Drew. For an instant, dark squinty eyes flashed with hate. Then the professional smile slid into place. Only his eyes stayed hard and cold. He strutted forward, hand outstretched, his rounded stomach extending over his fancy belt buckle.

"Well, well, well. If it isn't my esteemed opponent."

There was no way to avoid the pudgy fingers or the wet clasp of his grip. Despite his slight paunch and that double chin, Frederick Thane wasn't a big man. At least not yet. At fifty-five or thereabouts, he still had deep black hair, probably due to a little chemical assistance, and he was taller than Drew remembered. Lifts, Drew decided. Even so, the other man still had to look up to meet Drew's eyes, which obviously rankled.

"Mayor," he greeted.

"Saw your name on the other sign-up sheet." He shifted his rifle and stared at the handgun case. "We aren't competing in the same category." He swiped at the rivulets of sweat running down the sides of his face with a crumpled blue handkerchief.

"Not this time."

Thane's lips pursed tightly, as though he was trying to decide if there was another meaning beneath those words. "Hot enough for you?"

"I imagine it will get hotter before there is a winner."

Thane's eyes narrowed. "Count on it."

They were not talking about the weather or the contest. It was no secret that Frederick Thane was furious over Drew's decision to run against him. Thane had scared off every other opponent who dared consider throwing a hat in the ring for the mayoral election. Unfortunately for him, he didn't have any leverage to use against the Pierce family. Now he stared pointedly at Nancy Bell.

"And this must be the fancy publicist I heard your grandpa hired for you."

A sneer licked the edges of his words.

"Fancy?" he heard Nancy whisper to his brother. She sounded amused rather than annoyed.

"Nancy Bell, Frederick Thane," Drew introduced. "And you know my brother, Zach, of course."

"Of course, of course. Young Zach."

Zach winced visibly. He didn't offer to shake hands. Nancy, however, did. "Mayor Thane."

"Charmed, I'm sure."

Drew gave her points for neither shuddering at the contact of his damp hand nor wiping her own hand against her tailored light blue pants afterward.

"We fancy types are big on charm," she offered with a professional smile.

"You'll need it. You have your work cut out for you, my dear," Thane said.

"Hey, Drew, they're calling our party now," Zach interjected.

"Don't let me keep you," Thane said with false joviality. "I hear you're giving the family speech at the picnic in a few days. I'm looking forward to it."

"Are you? Then I guess I'll see you on the dais."

"Indeed you will. Ms. Bell. Young Zach." Thane pivoted away.

"If he called me 'young Zach' one more time I was going to try a little target shooting right out here," Zach muttered.

"Wouldn't be worth the cost of the bullets," Drew told him.

"So that was Frederick Thane," Nancy mused.

"In the flesh."

"Of which he has plenty," Zach added unkindly.

"Interesting." Nancy watched the mayor stop to chat with some people nearby. "He did make one valid point, you know. You don't really need me if he's your competition."

Zach barked a laugh.

"Don't let his bumpkin imitation fool you," Drew warned. "He's smart enough in his way. He's been running this town for a number of years now."

"And he'll do just about anything to keep that position and win this campaign," Zach added.

"I've studied his dossier," Nancy agreed. "But the man has a definite problem with his public image."

"What public image?" Zach demanded. "The man's a leech and everyone knows it. He's been sucking the town dry for years."

"But he keeps getting elected," she pointed out.

"Hard to lose when you're the only candidate," Zach said. "Everyone else has a habit of dropping out before the election."

"I believe lack of funds is usually cited," Nancy agreed. "But that won't be the case this time, will it, Andrew?"

Drew made a noncommittal sound and moved forward to check them in. No, funding definitely wouldn't be a problem, but he had no intention of dropping out of this race for any reason.

After helping Nancy select a gun to use, he looked around in irritation. "Where the heck is Carey?"

Carey Eldrich had coerced, begged, pleaded and even insisted they participate in the tournament. Once he explained to Nancy that practically the entire town turned out for the event, and that the tournament had started drawing people from as far away as Salem, she readily agreed Drew's participation was necessary.

"Sounds like a good place for some unofficial campaigning," she told him. "Before the Fourth of July kickoff I want you seen all over town participating in local events. I'll make sure you get plenty of media coverage. That's my job."

"And I'll bet you're very good at your job," Carey had said flirtatiously. "Just don't expect his picture on the front page as the winner of the tournament. I've been out-shooting him for years."

"Really?"

"Only if you count his mouth," Drew had told her.

So here they were, guns in hand. Everyone except Carey.

"You know Carey," Zach said. "He's probably talking to someone."

"You mean some woman," Drew said in annoyance.

"Of course. Want me to go and find him?"

"No need, Zach." Nancy pointed a peach-tipped fingernail. "Here he comes now."

Carey Eldrich rushed up, his blond good looks strangely flushed. His shirt was sweaty and plastered to his body. A worried expression deepened the furrow between his eyebrows.

"Out jogging?" Drew asked critically.

"Sorry," he offered sheepishly. "Something I ate this morning didn't agree with me."

Annoyance changed to concern. Drew stared at the man who had been his best friend and chief rival since grade school. As owners of the local newspaper, Carey's family was almost as prominent as the Pierce family. Drew figured he knew Carey about as well as anyone. Carey had been a ladies' man since conception, so Drew had to concede it was unusual for him to disappear when there was a beauty like Nancy on the scene. Especially when Carey had been competing with Drew for her attention ever since they'd met.

"Do you want to go home?" he asked his friend.

"No, no. I'm fine now. Besides, I promised to teach this lovely lady how to shoot. I want her to see for herself that I wasn't bragging last night. Out-shooting Drew is really as easy as I claimed," he told her archly.

But his tone was falsely hearty. Drew frowned. Before he could pull his friend aside to find out what was wrong, his attention centered on a woman with a mass of red-gold hair spilling over delicate shoulders. The woman stood with her back to him, talking intently to a man he didn't recognize. The graceful curve of her back and the tantalizing flare of slim hips encased in well-worn jeans anchored his attention.

He willed her to turn around. His stomach knotted as he waited for a glimpse of her face. Instead, she laid a hand on the man's bare arm. He in turn smiled intimately down at her. Drew took an unconscious step toward her.

The man's baseball cap masked his features, but Drew glimpsed silver-streaked hair poking from beneath his cap. The man looked to be in his fifties. What was Brianna doing with a man old enough to be her father? Hadn't she learned anything from what had happened to his sister?

Carey nudged him in the ribs. "What do you think, Drew?"

"What?" Momentarily diverted, his gaze whipped back to his companions.

"Fat chance," Zach responded to some comment Drew hadn't heard.

Carey's features lit in familiar challenge. "You want to take me on as well, Zach?"

"No way. I just want to watch the fun."

Irritated at the interruption, Drew turned back toward the woman, certain it was Brie. But the couple was strolling away, deep in conversation. The man's arm lay possessively across her shoulders as he bent his head close to hers in an intimate way. Drew clenched his jaw.

"Come on, we're up," Zach said.

As the couple faded into the crowd he reluctantly joined the others. Target shooting was the last thing Drew wanted to do—especially now. His reaction to seeing Brie was surprising. He'd known the possibility existed when he returned home to run for mayor, but he hadn't been prepared for the wild surge of emotions that bubbled inside him at the sight of a stranger's arm on her shoulders.

Maybe it hadn't been her.

Who was he trying to kid? Four years or forty, he suspected she would always incite emotions so elemental they gripped him like a vise. Brianna Dudley was the only female who had ever had the power to scramble his brains. How had he managed to forget that about her?

Edgy and out of sorts, he followed the others onto the range absently, lost in memories he'd put aside a long time ago. He jerked back to the present when he saw they'd been assigned to the last four stands on the end closest to the woods.

The firing range itself was built into a bowl-shaped depression surrounded by dense woods on three sides. He stared at the trees. The disquiet he'd been feeling all morning intensified. While a credible shot, Drew hadn't been able to summon up any enthusiasm for this tournament. Instead, his desire to leave was strong enough to surprise him.

"Something wrong, Drew?" Nancy asked as Carey took the stand beside him.

"No."

Carey eyed him strangely. Zach frowned. "Come on, Nancy, you're between me and Carey," he told her. "I'll help you get set."

"Oh, no, I'll help her," Carey said smoothly. "After all, I promised to show her how it was done."

Drew tuned them out. He gazed at the target downrange. It had been almost four years since he'd seen

Brie, yet she could still set his pulses racing from a distance. How crazy was that?

He sought another focus for his wandering attention. The brooding string of trees on the hill offered nothing helpful. He was here to compete. Inattention on a firing range was dangerous and stupid.

The call went out that the line was live. As people began firing their practice shots, the scent of cordite filled his nostrils. Blue clouds of smoke already hung in the heavy air. Shots thundered in his ears despite the requisite protective headgear. Sweat gathered at his hairline, beginning a lazy trickle down his face. He checked and loaded his weapon.

Drew lined up his sights and fired, wishing he were elsewhere—preferably an air-conditioned elsewhere, but Nancy had mapped out an entire program of places he needed to go over the next few days even though the real campaigning wouldn't begin until after the July Fourth festivities. With his father's blessing, Nancy had met with the float committee to discuss Drew's role on the family float. She'd scheduled him to give the short speech before the picnic, a job his grandfather and father generally handled, and she'd lined up a press interview immediately afterward.

His family had been right. She was good at her job. She'd done her homework on Moriah's Landing and she'd planned a solid strategy for getting his name in front of the community.

She was extremely attractive, and more than once he'd caught a hint of sensual awareness slumbering in her serious gaze. He gave her points for the subtle way she made her interest in deepening their relationship clear without coming on to him. They had a lot in common. Drew genuinely liked Nancy. She'd make a good political partner, but as tempting as she was, Drew hesitated to change their status. Resisting his family's attempts at matchmaking had become a habit. He knew his father and grandfather had decided Nancy was an ideal choice for more than his campaign manager.

Drew watched as she took careful aim at her target. Her first two shots went wide. The next shot hit the black outline on the outermost fringe. Carey had talked her into competing in the novice category even though she's said she'd never done any shooting before.

Because he was concentrating on Nancy, he never saw the figure pelting down the steep dirt incline until he turned back to take aim at his own target. He released the trigger instantly.

She ran like a puppet on a string—or someone at the tail end of their stamina. Her long, dark hair tangled around her face, hiding her features.

Drew yelled for everyone to hold their fire. But at the opposite end of the range, someone was shooting what sounded like a cannon. His voice had no hope of carrying over that sound.

Drew didn't stop to think. He sprinted toward the woman.

She stumbled and fell, taking his heart down with her. In seconds she was up again, but staggering.

A barrage of bullets passed so close Drew could practically feel the displaced air. The woman jerked to an abrupt stop. She twisted to look behind her, her features contorted by a mask of sheer panic. She took a faltering step and went down again. This time she made no move to rise.

He reached her, crouching over her still form. Red blossomed on her dirt-stained, cotton-print blouse. The deep, dark color spread rapidly across her chest. He sought for the pulse in her neck. Weak. Thready. He could hear each ragged breath she took. The shallow bursts sounded as if each one might be her last.

Her head lolled to the side, giving him a clear glimpse of the red furrow that had plowed its way along the side of her skull, disappearing beneath her tangled hair. Without moving her, he couldn't tell if the bullet had entered her head or not, but she was still alive.

The sudden silence was almost as deafening as the noise had been. Drew raised his face to yell for an ambulance.

Pressed against the fence at the top of the hill, Dr. Leland Manning drilled him with a stare of absolute hatred.

Shocked, Drew took a second to realize how the scene must look to the man. He was crouched over the woman's body, gun in hand.

Footfalls pounded up to him, snapping the spell. Voices shouted. People surrounded him, with more rushing forward. Carey Eldrich elbowed him aside, squatting beside the woman.

"Ursula?"

Of course. Ursula Manning, Leland Manning's beautiful new young wife.

"Don't move her," Drew cautioned, feeling ill.

The words came too late. Carey cradled her against his chest and stood. Blood streaked his arm, smearing his shirt.

"Where's the ambulance?" Carey roared. He ran with her, trailing a path of bright red droplets in his wake. Drew glanced over his shoulder up the hill. Leland Manning was gone.

Bits of excited, disjointed conversation bounced

around and through him as Drew rose unsteadily. He pushed his way through the crowd, following Carey.

"…call an ambulance?"

"…still alive?"

"Who is it?"

"…anyone called the…?"

"What was she doing out there?"

And that last question stuck in his head. An excellent question. What had Ursula Manning been thinking to run onto a live firing range like that? And where had she come from? Had she been running from her husband?

Someone gripped his forearm. He realized it was being shaken hard in an attempt to get his attention. Nancy Bell swam into focus. Her wide, pale eyes looked enormous. She looked from him to the gun still clutched in his hand.

"Oh, my God, Drew. Do you think you killed her?"

Chapter Two

Yesterday, news of the shooting had reached the diner less than half an hour after Brie started her shift. Details had been vague and wildly exaggerated as usual, but Brie couldn't imagine anyone, let alone the perfectly behaved Andrew Pierce, standing on the gun range with an Uzi submachine gun.

He was back in town to stay. Excitement warred with fear. She tried to tell herself it didn't matter. In four years he'd only made one halfhearted attempt to contact her after he left town for graduate school. Still, she was extremely thankful she'd left the firing range when she had. What if she'd run into Drew there?

Her heart gave a foolish lurch. Not that it had been likely, given the size of the crowd.

She hadn't slept much last night as a result of her chaotic thoughts and today she had agreed to pull a double shift. Tiredly, she lifted the laden serving tray. The diner had been filled since she'd come on duty. People stopped by for a quick bite or something to drink or simply to share the news with anyone who hadn't yet heard about yesterday's incident at the gun range. The town had seen too much of this sort of excitement lately. Evil seemed to have set up housekeeping in Moriah's Landing.

Three women had been murdered since the start of the year, their bodies brutally displayed for her friend, Elizabeth Douglas Ryan, to discover. Then, when a stalker went after another of her friends, Katherine "Kat" Ridgemont, people learned that the town's prodigal son, Jonah Ries, was an undercover FBI investigator looking into the secret society that most of the local scientists were rumored to belong to. And now Jonah and Kat planned to marry. While happy for Kat, Brie couldn't understand what was happening to their once peaceful town.

She set burgers and fries in front of Dodie and Razz. The local youths delighted in their reputation as the terrors of the neighborhood. Hard to believe Razz was her age. Even harder to believe that she had once accepted a date with him. She hated waiting on him and he knew it.

Normally, the two hung out at the arcade, but occasionally they came in for a sandwich. They were rude, noisy and never tipped. Razz liked to leer at her because he knew it made her angry, but he was careful not to take it any further than that. He hadn't forgotten how successfully she'd fought him off that night in his car any more than she had. And she'd made it perfectly clear she'd do a lot worse if he bothered her again.

She suspected the pair were behind a lot of the mischief that had been going on here at the waterfront. It defied logic that they hadn't been caught doing something illegal by now.

"That was a lot of blood, man," Dodie was saying.

"Arterial blood," Razz agreed, knowingly. "Bet she didn't survive the ambulance run."

"Think they'll arrest Drew Pierce?"

A chill snaked down her back.

Razz gave his younger friend a hard shove.

"Don't be stupid," Razz growled. "Nobody touches the almighty Pierce family. Besides, there were lots of witnesses who can claim it was the woman's own fault."

"Including us," Dodie said smugly.

"Shut up, stupid." Razz gave him another shove and a kick under the table. Deliberately, he stared hard at Brie. "We didn't get there until it was all over."

He was lying, and boldly daring her to contradict him. Brie was tempted. She wouldn't put much past the pair. Not even an accidental murder.

"Will there be anything else?" she asked politely.

"Yeah. Ketchup," Razz sneered.

She picked up the bottle sitting inches from his left hand and plopped it in front of him. Without another word she turned away.

What she wouldn't give to be able to go home and put her feet up. Maybe then her head would stop pounding. Then again, probably not. What she needed was sleep—something she hadn't been able to achieve after talking with her mother's doctor yesterday. His confirmation of her worst fears had left her too upset to even cry. Her mother was dying and there wasn't a thing anyone could do.

Research was being done here in Moriah's Landing, but clinical trials were a long way off yet. Even if the experimental procedure had been available, Brianna didn't know how she could possibly pay for anything not covered by her mother's medical plan. Last semester she'd gone back to college again for the first time since dropping out, determined to complete her degree. But

if her mother's medical bills were about to escalate, Brie
didn't see how she could continue. She'd need to pur-
chase school supplies next month with money she didn't
have yet.

Going home early wasn't an option today or any
other day.

She pushed at another strand of hair drooping moistly
against her forehead. A shorter style would be so much
easier to manage. Maybe she'd ask her mother to help
her chop some of it off tonight. Good haircuts were
expensive—another luxury she couldn't afford.

Rubbing her temple, she walked over to the booth
where Rebecca Smith stared vacantly at a menu. A new-
comer to town, Becca worked at Threads, the seamstress
shop over on Main Street. Brie had been immediately
drawn to the quiet woman the moment they met. The
attractive blonde appeared to be close to her own age
and Brie missed the tight-knit friendship she'd shared
with Drew's sister, Tasha, Elizabeth Ryan, Kat Ridgemont and Claire Cavendish. Even though Elizabeth and
Tasha lived on the wealthy side of town, the five women
had become close friends over the years. Tasha's death
five years ago, when her fiancé's boat exploded, had hit
them all hard. Especially since it had come on the heels
of Claire's abduction from St. John's Cemetery the
night of their college hazing.

Brie had never forgiven herself for allowing Claire
to go inside the haunted mausoleum that night. They
had all been scared, but Claire was the sensitive one,
the one least able to fend for herself. Brie had always
been stronger and street-smart. Maybe she could have
fended off the person who kidnapped, then tortured poor
Claire. But Claire had drawn the marked piece of paper
and had insisted on going through with the ritual. And

she had gone insane as a result of what had happened
to her. Claire was better now, even living at home once
more, but Brie wasn't sure she would ever fully recover.
They may not have seen the legendary Leary's ghost
that night, but he'd cursed them just the same.

While Brie's friends stopped by the diner periodi-
cally, they were all living vastly different lives now.
Elizabeth was happily married to Cullen Ryan, and Kat
had finally captured the attention of Jonah Ries. Brie
was honestly happy for her friends, but she was a bit
envious all the same.

"Hey, Brie," Becca greeted.

Brie smiled back. "Hey, yourself."

"Is it true? Was someone killed out at the firing range
yesterday?"

Brie shrugged unhappily. "That's what everyone is
saying."

"You didn't see it happen?"

"No, thank heavens. I wasn't there very long."

"I heard Andrew Pierce was involved. Isn't he the
man who's going to run against Mayor Thane?"

"Yes," she admitted, reluctant to think, let alone talk
about Drew. "What can I get you today?"

Fortunately, as the bell over the door continued to
chime, she had little time to chat. The day stretched on,
but at least she was busy. Brie collected dirty dishes
from a vacated booth, pocketing a generous tip gratefully. People were still waiting to be seated so she hurried. As she turned around her tray struck a passing arm.

She tried to steady the load, but a glass tipped,
splashing her with the remains of a soda and ice. Hands
suddenly steadied the tray from the other side. Dishes
clattered together. Total catastrophe was narrowly
averted.

She looked up and her words of thanks lodged in her throat. Instead of dishes, it was her world that came crashing down around her feet. People, sounds, even the heat faded away as she stared at the man holding the other side of her tray. Pain splintered the fragile wall she'd erected around her memories.

He wasn't supposed to be here. Not here in the diner. This was her part of town!

Andrew Pierce's impossibly brilliant blue eyes stared at her in shock.

"Brie?"

The sound of her name on his lips raised a lump of longing at the back of her throat. Drew stood there and she couldn't utter a sound.

"What are you doing here?" he asked.

His incredulous expression made it a whole lot easier to swallow the emotions churning inside her. She sensed his pity and that steadied her. Conscious of the room full of people, she settled for a terse reply.

"I work here. What are you doing? Out slumming?"

Again fluttered unspoken in the heavy air.

Dusky red climbed his neck.

Good. How dare he come here now? See her like this? In her fantasies they met one day in Salem or Boston or some other big city where she was a respected attorney. She would, of course, be perfectly dressed and not at all troubled by the sight of the only man she had ever loved.

His eyes narrowed. She couldn't help but notice that his thick black lashes were still tipped with gold—just like her daughter's.

"I came to see if the diner still carries that incredible blackberry pie," Drew said bitterly.

If he'd slapped her, she couldn't have been more hurt.

Her hands trembled and the dishes clattered, threatening to fall once more. Memories of sharing blackberry pie and long conversations with Drew were painfully raw.

"I'm sorry," he said so softly she wouldn't have heard the words if she hadn't seen his lips move.

"Andrew?"

Long, slender fingers rested against the skin of his lightly tanned bare arm. Brie felt as though those perfectly manicured nails had stabbed her soul. She hadn't realized Drew wasn't alone. She followed the nails up the arm to the face of the lovely woman at his side and discovered there were two curious men at his back, as well.

"Hello," the woman said in a deep, pleasant contralto. "I'm Nancy Bell, Andrew's…publicist."

"Really?" The back of her throat actually ached. "How nice for both of you. Trying to change his image should prove quite a challenge. Have a seat and someone will be with you in a moment."

"Ouch!" she heard Carey Eldrich exclaim.

"What on earth did you do to her, big brother?" Zachary Pierce demanded.

Brie didn't hear his reply. She pushed her way clear, the dishes rattling dangerously. Drew's stare burned a hole in her back all the way out to the hot, noisy kitchen where she nearly collided with Lois, the other waitress on duty.

"Whoa there!"

"Sorry."

"Hey, kid, you look awful."

"Thanks." Just what she wanted to hear.

"You're supposed to serve that stuff, not shower in it. Let me have the tray. That headache's really getting to you, isn't it?"

At the reminder, her headache returned with gleeful malice.

"Would you do me a favor, Lois? Another party just came in and I need to go take something. Would you cover their table for me?"

"Sure, kid. If you're going to break down and take medication that must be some headache. You want to go home? I can probably manage alone. I think we've already fed the town twice over."

More than anything in the world she wanted to go home.

"Thanks, Lois, but I'll be fine. If you'd just take the new table…"

"Sure. Why don't you go to the office and rest for a couple of minutes?"

"I'm okay."

And she would be. Eventually. It was just the shock of seeing him again like that when she hadn't expected it. What was he doing here? Why here of all places?

And why did seeing him again still have to hurt so much?

She refused to hide. It wasn't like she could change into someone other than a tired waitress. But taking a few minutes to wipe off the sticky cola and pull herself together wasn't hiding. And running a brush through her wild tangle of hair was hardly primping. She didn't bother replacing the makeup the heat had melted away hours ago.

She'd take a pain reliever and go back out front, hold her head up and do her job. She had nothing to be ashamed of. She wasn't a lawyer, but she was an excellent waitress.

If only were the saddest words she knew.

She swallowed two pain relievers dry and leaned her

head against the cool metal filing cabinet, closing her eyes. But that only sharpened the images from the past.

Drew, laughing down at her.

Drew, flirting with her.

Listening to her.

Hungry for her.

Kisses hotter than any fire. Hands that sought—then found. Incredible sensations. Pleasure and need so explosively raw it trembled on the edge of the world.

The moan startled her.

Her moan. And with it came a longing so poignant it brought the threat of tears even closer.

''What am I doing?''

She straightened away from the filing cabinet. Nearly four years and the memories were still so vivid they could make her moan out loud. Her eyes burned with foolish tears. She would not let him do this to her. Never again. Drew was yesterday. Brie lived in today. Family, work, school—this was her reality.

Squaring her shoulders, she took several deep breaths until she could shut off the past. She had given her word and she wasn't going to break it now. Andrew Pierce was out of her league and out of her life. While she couldn't pretend he was just another male, she could go out there and face him without collapsing. Everything would be okay.

As long as Drew never learned that he was the father of her child.

No one must ever learn that secret. She would die before she'd lose her daughter to the mighty Pierce family.

''I'M SORRY, WHAT DID YOU SAY?''

Drew forced his attention back to Nancy and discovered she wasn't the only one watching him with speculative eyes.

"I asked you if she was an old girlfriend," Nancy said lightly.

"No. Just a friend." Girlfriends were women you took to concerts or movies or parties. You did more with a girlfriend than talk with them and walk with them and buy them an ice-cream cone. Sadly, that pretty much summed up his relationship with Brianna. He'd never taken her anywhere—except on the public beach.

That memory still had the power to shame him.

He'd been twenty-four, stifled by his family and all the demands being placed on him. The year after Tasha's death had been hard for all of them, and being home for an entire month that summer, at loose ends, edgy, angry, frustrated, he'd let Carey drag him to a party. He hadn't wanted to attend. It had felt wrong to laugh and have fun when his sister was dead. But once he'd seen Brianna standing across the room, he hadn't wanted to leave.

He'd definitely been a moth to the red-gold flame of her hair. He hadn't known, then, she was his sister's gawky, freckled-faced friend. There had been nothing gawky about Brianna that night. As if pulled by an invisible wire, he'd gone forward to cull her from the group, finding a relatively quiet corner where they could talk.

And talk they did. She was like no one he had ever met, laughing up at him with bright green eyes that sparkled with good-humored mischief.

Brianna. So vibrantly alive. The name had rippled in his mind, stirring the ghost of a memory, but he'd been too distracted to concentrate on anything besides her. She teased him over his stuffy manners, then vivaciously argued his family's more conservative views. She was bright, witty and incredibly easy to talk to. Best of all, she wasn't the least bit impressed at being in the company of a Pierce.

She had no idea what that alone was worth to him. She made him think, with her uncanny insight into people and actions. And she made him laugh—deep, honest laughter from the heart. And as the hours slipped away, he felt more freely alive than he had in a very long time.

She wouldn't let him take her home. She wouldn't give him her telephone number, not even when he used every ounce of his highly reputed charm. Brianna merely smiled. Drew had been convinced men would willingly die for that smile.

Shockingly, he'd wanted her, right there in the midst of that noisy crowd. He'd never had a jealous bone in his body until that night, but he realized he didn't want her sparkling like that in front of all those other panting males. He cut them off with a look. Especially Carey. His friend's reputation with women was legendary and Drew wanted Brianna all to himself.

He learned pathetically little about her that night. She was good at deflecting his questions. She was attending Heathrow College, determined to be a lawyer, but by the time she disappeared from the party, he'd wanted to know so much more. Brianna Dudley was a witch and Drew didn't mind in the least being firmly under her spell.

Until Carey pointed out why her name was familiar. Brianna was Brie, his sister's young friend! Since he hadn't spent much time at home over the past several years, there was no reason for him to recognize the gorgeous young woman she'd become. She was a local girl who lived with her mother on the other side of town by the wharf. She was attending the prestigious local college, but only because she'd received a full scholarship.

Somehow, having been Tasha's friend put Brianna out of bounds. But it didn't stop his attraction. Despite his resolve, he couldn't stay away from her. His family's potential displeasure if they found out about the relationship probably played at least a small part in the fact that he continued to see her—on a purely platonic basis.

He spent lots of time eating pie at the Beachway Diner. Brie flirted lightly and so did he, glad she never took him seriously. That made it a little easier to ignore the enticing curves of her body and the way she always smelled so clean and fresh.

It had been much harder to ignore the play of lights gleaming in her enticing hair. Back then it had hung in shimmery red-gold curls nearly to her waist. Her hair had practically begged his hand to tangle in its flames. Drew spent a lot of time taking cold showers that summer while trying not to imagine how all that hair would look spread across his naked chest.

Physical attraction aside, Brie knew how to listen. He liked that about her. In fact, he liked everything about her.

He had a lot of respect for the goals she'd set. She was bright and eager with big plans for her life. Plans that didn't include him, as she'd made perfectly clear the last time they had talked.

The memory was bitter even now. Not because she'd told him to get lost. He deserved much worse. He'd betrayed her trust. He'd betrayed his own honor. Worst, he'd hurt a valued friend.

Drew grit his teeth in regret. He couldn't undo the

past, but seeing her here today, he needed to understand. Why was Brie still serving customers instead of justice? What had become of all her dreams and plans? For some reason it felt important that he understand.

"Don't let him kid you," Carey was telling Nancy. "Drew had the hots for Brianna one summer. Then he found out she was just a kid. And from the wrong side of town at that."

"She isn't a kid anymore," Nancy said.

"No. She sure isn't," Carey said thoughtfully.

Drew nearly leaned across the table with his fist. The primitive urge to turn that handsome face to pulp surprised him, particularly when it didn't go away. He had to force his fingers to unclench.

"This is a very nice side of town," Drew enunciated in a deadly soft tone of voice. "People who live over here don't need expensive cars and lots of money to have a good time. They understand what's really important."

Carey blinked. His lips parted as the barb slid home. Zach perked up in his seat, alert to his brother's shift in mood. Only Nancy appeared puzzled.

"Aw, hell." Carey said. "You still have the hots for her, don't you?"

"Don't say another word, Carey."

Carey clamped his mouth closed. Drew slid out of the booth and stood.

"Where are you going?" Nancy asked in concern.

"I need some air."

"But you haven't eaten yet."

"I'm not hungry."

"Please sit down, Drew. We don't want a scene. And we didn't come here for the food, anyhow, if you'll recall."

He stepped out of reach of the hand she moved toward him. "No scenes. And there's nothing wrong with my memory. I just don't feel like campaigning right now. Excuse me."

He strode outside without looking back. He was very much afraid if he did, he'd give in to his desire to grab Carey and use his friend's face to relieve some of the tension roaring inside him.

Hazy, late afternoon heat shimmered in the air. The boardwalk teemed with people. From skimpy scraps of material daring to be called bathing suits, to the colorful garb worn by a local fortune-teller, people strolled and chatted gaily—in direct contrast to his somber mood.

Wheels, a bar a few doors down, opened to disgorge a tall black man in a biker uniform. Music blared at decibels that couldn't possibly be good for the human ear. Drew changed direction. A cold beer suddenly appealed far more than a club sandwich and fries.

The biker gave him a hard stare. Drew's expression must have been as fierce as his thoughts, because the man deliberately flexed his fingers and waited. Anticipation hummed through him. If this joker was looking for a fight, Drew was in the perfect mood to accommodate him. He hadn't been in a brawl since—

"The last time you made that mistake, she paid the price."

Drew pivoted, startled. The fortune-teller, known as Yvette, stood on the sidewalk only a few feet away, watching him with a fathomless expression.

"Excuse me?"

"You won't find answers in the bottom of a bottle. Nor in a barroom brawl."

His insides twisted. People passed between them. The

seer didn't move. Her utter stillness was uncanny. So was her knowledge of what he'd been thinking.

"Can I help you with something?" he finally asked.

She let out a troubled sigh. Almost reluctantly, she shook her head. Her thick, dark hair was as long as Brie's had been that summer.

"No," she replied sadly. "Nor can you help her. Not yet."

"What are you talking about?"

"I wonder if she remembers that a kiss can break the spell," she muttered under her breath.

A fruitcake. He hadn't heard that about her, but that crazy outfit and all the jewelry she wore should have tipped him off. No one in their right mind would dress like that on a day like this.

"The beach is crowded," she continued. "Still, a walk might clear your head. You've made a serious enemy, Mr. Pierce. Tread with caution."

So she knew who he was. She probably also knew what had happened at the gun range yesterday. Did she think he'd killed Ursula Manning as Leland Manning seemed to believe?

A noisy group of teenagers cut between them, laughing and jostling one another as they passed. He followed the orange and green swirl of her skirt as the gypsy trailed the group into the busy diner without another word.

He was tempted to go after her and demand an explanation. Only what sort of explanation could he expect from a crazy person?

Besides, Brie was inside. For several long seconds he stood there uncertainly, more unnerved by the gypsy's strange words than he wanted to admit.

The biker had given up the wait. He pulled out of the

parking lot with a roar. Drew headed for the bar. At the last moment, he walked on past, heading for the entrance to the public beach.

The sand writhed with tan bodies, loud music and yelling children. The scent of water and suntan lotion mingled in the heavy, hot air. There wasn't even a breeze to stir the mix together.

Had there been a breeze that night four years ago?

Drew couldn't remember. Jake and Rider, two Vietnam veterans and co-owners of Wheels, had thrown him out after his second beer. Antihistamines and beer had made his head swim dizzily as he staggered to his car that night. His fingers had struggled to make the key fit in the lock without success.

Brie had appeared at his side, still wearing her uniform. Her hair had been slipping from its haphazard knot on top of her head, and he was pretty sure she wasn't wearing a trace of makeup. Yet he'd wanted her with devastating intensity. It had been awfully hard to remember just then why he couldn't have what he wanted.

He'd gone all gruff and macho when she'd tried to get him to go into the diner for a cup of coffee. He'd turned back to the car and dropped the keys. Brie had snatched them up, refusing to give them to him. When he tried to grab them from her, she took off running.

That had been all the stimulus he'd needed. He could still remember how his body sang with desire as he chased her down these rickety wooden steps. Stumbling, lurching across the empty sand, he'd wanted her more with each breath. So he caught her, tumbling them both down against a still-warm dune.

She'd tasted of pie and woman and she'd kissed him back with a hunger that had first startled, then stoked his ego enormously. He couldn't get enough of her mouth. She strained against him, incredibly soft.

He hadn't known. Hadn't even suspected the truth. Brianna hadn't kissed like a virgin. She'd kissed like a woman who knew exactly what she wanted. And she'd wanted him.

If she'd told him to stop he was pretty sure he could have. He liked to think he would have despite his condition. But she didn't tell him to stop and his hands and his mouth had separated from his fuzzy brain.

Drew closed his eyes against the memory, but he could feel a swell of passion as clearly as if it were happening right now. The lush roundness of her breasts when he'd unbuttoned her uniform and pushed up her bra. The heady reaction to his mouth on her tender skin. She'd been so wild. A match to the tinder of his desire.

Maybe if he hadn't mixed the drugs with the beer… but the combination hadn't been nearly as potent as her mouth. He'd been wanting her for so long.

His hand tightened on the wood railing. In the dark, on that very public beach, he'd succumbed to primitive urges and claimed her innocence. Drew inhaled, surprised to find his body all but shaking at the memory. To this day, he couldn't remember anything after that stunning shock and the incredible, mind-blowing pleasure of his own release. He had no idea how he got back to his car, or how Brie had gotten home.

One more ghost to prod his conscience.

He'd awakened hours later, alone and cramped, inside his car, sand all over his clothing. His keys had dangled from the ignition. If it hadn't been for the lingering scent and taste of her, he would have told himself he dreamed the entire scene.

Guilt had been his harsh companion driving through

the empty streets that morning. He had showered and changed, returning to the diner as soon as he could get away without complicated explanations.

If he lived to be a million he would never forget the smile of her greeting, or the way it had withered and died when he'd sputtered out an apology.

Brianna Dudley had haunted him for four years and he hadn't realized how much until just now. He stared at the murky horizon and tried to force his stiff muscles to relax.

"You should take off your shoes."

"What?" Drew looked down and found a small boy staring up at him.

"If you're going walking on the beach you should take off your shoes. Otherwise they get sand in them and they feel yucky."

The boy pushed at the bridge of his wire-framed glasses and regarded Drew solemnly.

"Yucky, huh? Isn't the sand hot on your feet?"

The boy nodded.

"Then I guess I won't walk down there after all." Not even if the urge to see if that dune was still there was eating a hole inside him. The dune was probably gone, anyhow, or at least changed beyond recognition. And even if he recognized it, so what? He couldn't undo the past.

But maybe he could find out why the present hadn't changed. Maybe instead of a walk on the beach, he'd take a walk up the hill to where the clapboard houses sat like little boxes. If he was going to run for mayor he should see how his constituents on this side of town were coping with their lives.

Chapter Three

Reflected in the late afternoon haze, the houses appeared shabbier than he remembered, the neighborhood more run-down. The narrow cobblestone street was in bad need of repair. Yet flowers bloomed, even though most had a wilted look, as if they, too, struggled to survive.

Drapes were drawn tightly, doors and windows shut against the heat, adding to the neglected air. Even the noisy hum of window air conditioners didn't detract from the deserted appearance. The late afternoon sun baked the neighborhood without the faintest whiff of a breeze.

Drew paused beneath the drooping leaves of a tall, gnarled tree that rose from the withered ground at the curb of the only house sporting open doors and windows. More weeds than grass covered the ratty lawn, while scraggly, misshapen bushes hid the peeling paint that covered the front porch with its sagging steps and broken railing. Brianna's house. Or it had been. Did she and her mother still live here?

A group of young children in bathing suits suddenly erupted around the corner. Squeals split the depressing silence.

Rooted to the spot, Drew watched as the group clattered noisily up the steps. The screen door opened and a woman who could have been Brianna's twin sister stepped outside. Only, Brianna didn't have a twin sister. She also didn't have a daughter, but the tiny little redheaded urchin leading the pack was definitely related.

The woman bent down and laughed at something the child said. She wiped at a smudge of dirt with a motherlike flick of her thumb. The resemblance between the three was extraordinary.

Did they share the same intriguing spray of freckles across their faces?

The miniature Brianna threw her arms around the woman's neck while the other four children chattered excitedly. High-pitched giggles completely destroyed the gloomy silence of the neighborhood. As the woman ushered the group inside, her gaze came to rest on him.

Now that he saw her features more clearly, he recognized Pamela Dudley. Old enough to be Brie's mother, she was also young enough to have a three-or four-year-old daughter, he realized. The man he'd seen with Brie yesterday must have been her father.

Pleased at that thought, he became aware that the woman continued to stare at him. Exactly the sort of protective look a mother might give a stranger out of place in her neighborhood and paying too much attention to her child.

He offered her a friendly nod and started walking, trying to look casual. Great. She probably thought he was a child molester. He should have gone over and introduced himself.

As what? Her daughter's first lover? The man who would be mayor? Drew lengthened his stride. He should have gone walking on the beach, after all. He only hoped Pamela Dudley didn't call the police. He'd spent enough time with the forces of law and order yesterday.

Detective Cullen Ryan had been thorough. Ursula Manning was dead. Accident or not, Ryan needed to determine who had fired the fatal shots and why the woman had been there in the first place. Drew had had to curb his temper more than once as he answered questions repeatedly. He had never even met the woman. But he understood Ryan's frustration. The man was a good cop and he had a job to do.

What *had* the woman been doing there?

Drew slowed his pace as he approached the corner where the crumbling brick strip club, Girls! Girls! and the Wharf Rat bar, shadowed the narrow sidewalk. This was not the greatest neighborhood to be raising a child. All sorts of unsavory types hung out down here.

When a figure suddenly stepped from the shadows of the bar, Drew's heart jumped, even as he recognized Leland Manning. At least those rumors of Manning being a vampire weren't true. Drew had seen him in daylight twice now, though both times those eerily cold eyes seemed to burn right through him.

"Dr. Manning," he greeted. "I didn't have an opportunity to offer my condolences yesterday. I really wish I could have reached your wife in time."

Drew stopped, stunned by the malice in those deepset eyes. In that instant, Drew had no trouble believing there was something unearthly about Leland Manning.

"You'll pay," Manning said coldly. "I'll see to it."

"Hey, I didn't kill your wife," Drew protested.

Manning strode past. Only then did Drew notice Jake Carpenter, co-owner of Wheels, standing on the sidewalk a few feet away.

"I was there yesterday," the ex-marine said gruffly.

"Damn fool thing, running out there like that. Only luck kept you from getting shot, too."

"Tell it to Manning," Drew said ruefully.

"Don't think that dude's of a mind to listen." Jake gazed after Manning and his features puckered into a frown. Drew found his own heart thudding unevenly. Manning had vanished.

The men exchanged uneasy looks. Manning could have stepped into one of the shops lining the street, but it seemed unlikely given the nature of those establishments. Come to think of it, why would a grieving widower be in this neighborhood the day after his wife's death?

"Guy's weird," Jake muttered.

Privately, Drew agreed. He didn't know Manning, though his Uncle Geoff did.

"Hard to picture someone like him married to a woman like Ursula Manning."

Drew rubbed his jaw, nodding in agreement. He still expected Manning to step out of one of the shops.

"Cops know what she was doin' there?" Jake asked conversationally.

Drew turned his attention back to the beefy biker. "If they do, they aren't saying."

But Ursula Manning had been scared. Drew had seen her look toward the line of trees right before she fell. David Bryson had been lurking in those trees only a short time earlier—a fact Drew had been only too happy to share with the police.

So had Leland Manning.

"At least ballistics will show who fired the fatal shots," Jake said. "That should change Manning's attitude."

"Hopefully." While all the weapons had been confiscated for testing, in the confusion immediately following the shooting, things had been pretty muddled. It was possible the police had missed a gun or two.

"Understand Manning's wife was a nature photographer from Salem," Jake said thoughtfully. "Guess that might explain what she was doing in the woods, but you have to wonder what made her climb a clearly posted fence that way. She must have heard the gunfire."

He was right. Which meant she'd deliberately run toward the sound, probably looking for help.

Jake tipped his head, consideringly. "Buy you a beer?"

Touched by the unexpected offer, Drew shook his head. "I'd like that, but I have some people waiting for me over at the diner. Another time?"

"Sure. Stop by Wheels any time you're in the neighborhood."

Drew headed for the diner without catching a glimpse of Leland Manning. Carey was standing outside, hands thrust in his pockets. There was an unusual slump to his posture. He straightened as soon as he spotted Drew.

"Where'd you go?" Carey demanded.

"For a walk."

"In this heat? Are you nuts?"

"Drop it, Carey."

Carey raised his palms in surrender. "Sure. Consider it dropped." He sent a speculative gaze toward the bar. "Zach ran Nancy back to the estate. She's not too happy with you right now."

"She'll get over it."

"A little sweet talk wouldn't hurt. She kept muttering something about damage control."

"Nancy doesn't need sweet talk from me. She works for me, remember?"

"Whoa. You are in a mood. Uh, look, I'm sorry if I ticked you off inside. You aren't—you know—still interested in that waitress, are you? I mean, she's got…" Carey took a hasty step back. "Oh, hell."

"Don't say another word," Drew warned him. He couldn't see his friend's eyes, hidden behind dark sunglasses, but he sensed a whole stream of questions. Too bad. He didn't owe Carey or anyone else an explanation. He strode over to where they'd parked and waited for Carey to hit the button that unlocked the passenger door.

"When do I get my car back?" Drew asked as he slid inside the bright green sports car he'd lent Carey several weeks ago.

"My car's supposed to be out of the shop tomorrow if they get that part in. Do you need it before then?"

Drew shook his head. "Tomorrow's fine." He had other cars at his disposal.

They rode in silence, letting their private thoughts do the talking on the drive back to the Pierce compound. Carey pulled Drew's sports car up in front of the main house instead of parking.

"Aren't you coming in?" Drew asked.

"No. Thanks."

"Look, I'm sorry I jumped down your throat."

Carey regarded him soberly. "You know, don't you?"

His stomach plummeted. "Know what?"

"One of the four of us must have fired the shots that killed her."

BRIE WAS RELIEVED when she could finally take off her apron and head home a little early. Questions without answers had tormented her all evening as she took orders and waited tables. Andrew Pierce and the shooting were on everyone's lips, especially after the way he left the diner before his food arrived.

New rumors were circulating. One had Ursula Manning attacked by bears in the woods. Another said she'd been kidnapped and held for ransom. Rumors being a way of life, Brie didn't put much stock in any of them, but she did wonder about Drew's abrupt departure. Seeing him again wasn't supposed to be so traumatic. She wasn't supposed to care anymore. Only, she had missed Drew and their long conversations over pie and coffee.

She'd always known he was going to be someone important in politics one day. He was so smart and he cared so much. And she'd used that knowledge to convince herself not to tell him about Nicole. Drew was an honorable man, who didn't need a scandal or an unacceptable wife and child just because she'd been a fool. Yet sooner or later someone would tell him she had a daughter. Drew wasn't stupid. He could do the math. Then what?

Why had he come to the diner today? People had long memories. Even without Carey's careless remark, someone was bound to remember the summer he'd hung out at the diner. What if that someone went to the media? Nicole's eyes were a dead giveaway to her parentage. Brie gripped her pad a little tighter.

A sense of helpless panic built inside her.

The residents of Moriah's Landing tended to live by very narrow, old-fashioned codes of behavior. They didn't hang women for being witches anymore or brand them with a scarlet letter, but they wouldn't condone a Pierce getting a young girl from the wrong side of town pregnant, and then abandoning her to her fate. It wouldn't matter to anyone that Drew hadn't known about the child. He'd be expected to know. The gossip would destroy him—and his budding career in politics.

Depressed by the course of her thoughts, Brie said good-night to her co-workers and stepped outside. Her mind still raced with "what if" images as the hot muggy air of the night enfolded her.

A summer storm was brewing. She could feel it pulsing over the water. Her mother had always said Brie was better than a barometer. She searched the dark sky. It would thunder soon.

Her steps faltered. A cluster of men stood at the far end of the sidewalk in the gap between Wheels and the Bait and Tackle shop.

Little light reached that stretch of sidewalk. Not enough to identify the men. She was about to cross the street when she recognized Razz's nasal voice. His words carried clearly, stopping her mid-stride.

"Pierce killed the Manning woman, all right, and who's to say it was really an accident?"

"You mean he shot her on purpose?"

"Think about it. A good-lookin' woman like that married to an old man? It'd be a heck of a clever way to get rid of an unwanted lover, don't you think?"

"You think she was messin' around with him?"

"Rider saw her get in Pierce's car one day."

"That don't mean nothing."

"I heard her wrists had marks like she'd been tied up," another voice dissented.

"Maybe Pierce is into S and M," someone else joked.

Brie knew she should keep walking. They were only gossiping like everyone else.

"Wait and see," Razz said. "Some other poor slob will take the fall for her death. No one can say for sure who was shooting with which gun. Makes for a nice clean murder."

"I don't know, man…"

"Me an' Dodie was there," Razz persisted. "The whole town saw Pierce standin' over her body. He looked guilty as sin. Nice, huh? We could elect ourselves a mayor who got away with murder."

Fury washed away her common sense. Brianna strode forward, the slap of her soles echoing hollowly on the cobblestone street. All four heads swiveled in her direction.

"Do you know the penalty for slander, *Edgar?*" she demanded, using his hated given name.

Razz bristled. He loomed tall and menacing, but Brie refused to back down.

"Now, why do I have a feeling Mayor Thane paid you to spread that rumor? Must be because I saw him talking with you and Dodie out here a few hours ago. What's the going rate for malicious gossip, Edgar?"

She had seen the mayor stop his car in the street to talk with them shortly after Drew abruptly left the diner.

"Watch your mouth, little girl," he said.

"Does the truth hurt? You told *me* that you and Dodie didn't get there until after the shooting," she reminded him.

The three toughs looked from her to Razz. He bristled as he realized he was losing credibility.

"If you don't want to get hurt, move along. This here's a private conversation."

"On a public sidewalk," she fired back.

Her insides twisted at the sudden feral malice in his expression. Razz and trouble had always been synonymous. But even the night of her only date with him, she had never considered him dangerous.

Until now.

She should have kept her mouth closed and kept walking. But since she hadn't, she knew better than to let him see any trace of fear.

"Fair warning, Razz. I wouldn't make accusations like that so publicly if I were you," she warned.

"Good thing you aren't me, then."

The four of them crowded close enough for her to smell the beer they had consumed. Belatedly, her common sense kicked in. The storm was gathering speed, closing in like them. A darting glance around showed the normally busy street was hauntingly empty. Even senile Arabella Leigh, who liked to walk this part of town at all hours, was nowhere in sight. The loud music reverberating from inside the bar would cover any scream for help she might make.

No question. She was in trouble.

Brie focused on Razz. "If Andrew Pierce had been responsible for Ursula Manning's death, he would have said so," she stated calmly, thrusting her hands inside the pockets of her uniform so they couldn't see how badly she was shaking. "Yesterday was a tragic accident. Ursula ran onto the firing range during the tournament without warning. Drew tried to save her life."

"Yeah?" Razz reached out deliberately and stroked her hair. Reflexively, she jerked back before she could stop herself, provoking a satisfied smile. She managed a glare, hoping he couldn't hear the way her heart was trying to pound its way free of her chest.

"Didn't anyone ever teach you it isn't smart to interrupt a private conversation?" Razz sneered menacingly.

"Yeah, you might get hurt or something," the leering one added.

Her hand closed over the canister of mace she always carried. It was a small can. Nowhere near big enough to do her much good against four of them.

A dark shadow suddenly detached itself from the side of the bait shop.

"Is there a problem here?" a low voice asked quietly.

They whirled as one. David Bryson glided forward without a sound. He was dressed completely in black despite the heat, and there was something menacing in the uncanny way his features remained in shadow—as if he weren't quite real.

"Brianna?" he asked.

Brie inhaled in relief at the sight of Tasha's former fiancé, but she didn't release her grip on the canister of mace.

"Beat it," one of the toughs said.

"We're havin' a conversation," the leering one added.

But as he faced the shadowy form of David Bryson, the leer faded. He suddenly appeared younger and weaker than he had just a moment ago.

"Is that right?" David asked softly. His gaze went to her. "Brianna?"

The others tensed, waiting for her verdict. Only Razz looked angry. She had just made a dangerous enemy no matter how she answered.

"It's late," she enunciated carefully. "I'm through talking this evening."

"Yeah? Well, fine," the self-appointed spokesman agreed. "Me, too. Come on, guys. We'll see you around, Razz."

Her shock mingled with relief as the group headed

back inside the bar. Razz clenched his fists. He looked as if he wanted to protest, but after glancing at David he seemed to think better of what he'd been about to say.

"We'll finish our talk," he told her. "Another time."

"That wouldn't be advisable," David warned. He reached out, stopping Razz in his tracks. A shudder passed through the youth before he jerked free of that hand.

"What are you?" Razz demanded. "Her keeper?"

"If necessary."

"Yeah? Well, I'll keep that in mind," he said, struggling to regain some of his usual swagger.

"Do that...Edgar."

Razz tried for one last look of intimidation that failed miserably. David simply waited. Razz added a glare for Brie's benefit before sauntering toward the front door of the bar. Brie watched him go inside before she let herself relax.

"Thank you, David."

There was no answer. David Bryson had melted back into the shadows without a sound.

Trembling from head to toe, Brie turned blindly back to the street. She would have to hurry now to beat the storm. She sensed it gathering to make a push inland. Car headlights momentarily blinded her when she would have stepped into the street. A vehicle braked to a halt directly in front of her. Her mouth went dry with new fear as the driver's door burst open.

Andrew Pierce stepped into the street.

"Taxi?" he asked.

She tried to swallow. Surely her knees wouldn't fold on her now. Not now. Not in front of Drew. A delayed reaction, that's all it was. This weak, fluttery feeling had nothing to do with the fact he was standing a few feet away looking at her with boyish wistfulness.

"Wha-what are you doing here?"

"Offering you a ride home."

"I'd rather walk."

He came around the car. "I remember."

He said it so gently she felt an inexplicable need to cry.

"You always did like to walk."

Oh, God. His voice ran like a caress over nerves stretched too tight. She fought an urge to throw herself into his unsuspecting arms in relief.

"There's a storm coming in," he continued, "and you never carry an umbrella."

Why did he have to remember that? It wasn't fair. She didn't want to remember how thoughtful he could be. How could she ignore him with this longing welling up inside her all over again? Would she never outgrow her infatuation with Drew?

"Brie? Did something happen?" A new alertness came to his stance. His gaze swept her, the bar and the street, lingering on the dark shadows where David Bryson had stood only a few seconds ago. Drew couldn't have seen him, so he must be picking up on her nervousness.

Before she could respond, music blared stridently as the door to Wheels swung open. They turned at the sound. Razz stood silhouetted against the faint light filtering onto the street. Blood thundered in her head. She sensed his satisfaction even as he stepped back inside.

Drew looked from the bar to her. "Friend of yours?"

She shuddered. "Not in a zillion years."

His mouth firmed. He looked like a man ready for a

confrontation. Her hand lifted to stop him and then had nowhere to go as he turned to her instead.

"You shouldn't be walking out here alone at this hour." He glanced back at the bar. "It isn't safe. Get in the car, Brie. I'm taking you home. The weatherman says it could be a nasty storm."

She knew. But she was more afraid of another sort of storm altogether. One that didn't involve the weather. She should refuse and tell Drew to go. Right now Razz was probably inside with his friends spreading the news that she was out here talking to Drew.

He opened the passenger door.

A sudden cold wind gusted across the beach. Lightning forked the distant clouds. Brianna slipped inside the car.

As she sank into the plush leather seat she tried to tell herself this wasn't a mistake. Drew's car was blocking traffic—or would be if there had been any. She couldn't make a scene out here where anyone might see them. But now she was alone with Drew. Awareness enfolded her as he slid in beside her.

"New car?" she asked nervously. "Didn't you used to have a green sports car?" Thank heaven this was a larger sedan. His presence still managed to take too much of the oxygen from the close quarters.

"This is one of the family cars. I lent Carey my car last week. His is in for repairs."

"Oh." She couldn't think of anything else to say. A wind gust sent sand pelting against the car. Rain followed on its heels. Drew flicked the windshield wipers on high and put the vehicle in gear.

She stared at the rhythmic swish of the wipers to keep from staring at him. The scent of his aftershave was an unwelcome sensual assault on nerves already stretched too thin.

"You shouldn't be walking these streets after dark," he chided.

"When you get to be mayor you can pass a law," she told him dryly. "No walking after dark."

"So you heard about that."

"I work at gossip central—otherwise known as the Beachway Diner. Of course I heard you plan to run for mayor. Probably before you even made the decision to run."

He flashed her a grin and her heart stood still. How was it possible to feel so enervated, yet so completely aware all at the same time?

"I keep forgetting about the gossip mill," he said.

The wipers strained to clear the windshield. She didn't know how he could drive in this downpour. She couldn't see a thing. He flicked on the defroster and both hands gripped the steering wheel as wind rocked the car.

"What just happened back there?" he asked softly.

"Nothing."

He glanced at her but had to concentrate on the road. That gave her an opportunity to study the subtle changes in him. He'd always been incredibly handsome, but now youthful charm had surrendered to a far more formidable maturity. He exuded an inner confidence, as if he'd finally come to terms with who he was and where he was going.

The knowledge was bittersweet. She was glad for him, but sorry because it opened the gap between them to an impossible chasm she couldn't hope to breach.

"Brie?"

He pulled into her mother's driveway and stopped the car. His stare was as potent as a touch against her skin.

"*Was* someone hassling you tonight?"

"I made a mistake in judgment." A big one. "It won't happen again."

"Is that why you're shaking?"

She clasped her hands together tightly. "Your defroster is cold."

He switched it off.

"Thanks. And thanks for the ride," she added quickly.

His hand closed over her arm before she could find the handle to the door. The unexpected contact was electrifying. For a moment neither of them moved.

"Brianna." He breathed her name as if he, too, had been jolted. He shook his head quickly as if to clear it. "We need to talk."

"I can't."

"Why not? We used to talk all the time," he said gently. "Remember?"

Ridiculous tears stung her eyes. Defensively, she reached for sarcasm. "Sure, I remember," she managed to say lightly. "Do you want ice cream on that pie? Will it be coffee or soda today?"

His jaw set. The pulse in his neck quickened, making her ashamed.

"Please let go of my arm, Drew." What would she do if he refused? "It's late and I'm very tired."

He withdrew his hand slowly, trailing it over her skin. Her belly quivered. Wind-driven rain continued to beat against the car. He stared as if he were trying to see past her words to read her chaotic thoughts.

Oh, God. He could convey so much in a simple look. She'd dreamed about those remarkable eyes, but never once had she pictured them filled with a sadness that nearly matched her own.

"What happened, Brie?"

"I told you—"

"I don't mean tonight, though I want to know about that too. What happened to all your plans? Why are you working in the diner instead of a courtroom in Boston?"

She tried to summon anger, but his expression made that impossible. All she had to do was open the door and leave. Why couldn't she make her fingers cooperate?

"What are *you* doing here, Drew?"

"Trying to talk with you."

"We did all our talking a long time ago."

"Did we?" Holding her gaze he leaned forward, stroking the side of her face.

Brie quivered. She leaned into that caress without thought, automatically turning her face into his palm. It had been so long.

He leaned closer, until the seat belt brought him up short. Raising her chin with his fingers, he gazed at her. She felt his breath against her cheek. Her heart fluttered wildly in anticipation of his lips on hers once more.

Lightning flared, a catalyst that knifed through the chaos of her emotions.

"No!"

She jerked free. Drew sat back.

Then the windshield exploded outward in a clap of sound.

Chapter Four

In the instant it took his mind to process what had happened, his body was already reacting. "Get down!" Drew shouted. He tugged her across the seat and covered her body with his own.

Rain pelted the car. Thunder rumbled. He registered the sound of a car speeding away. By the time he lifted his head, there were only two red taillights disappearing in a blur.

Brie sat up slowly.

"Are you okay?" he demanded.

"I think so. What happened?"

He watched her puzzlement change to dawning comprehension and then horror as she stared at the hole in the windshield.

Drew reached for his cell phone.

"Wait! What are you doing?" She grabbed for the instrument.

"Take it easy. I'm calling the police."

"You can't!" She snatched the phone from his hand and tossed it over the seat.

"Why did you do that?"

"You can't call the police."

"Why not? Someone just shot at us." And he had a pretty good idea who that someone was.

"Don't you realize what will happen if it gets out you were here with me?"

Panic edged her voice up an octave. She was shaking, and he had to grip her arm to prevent her from getting out of the car. "What are you talking about?" Her eyes were wide, dark orbs. Getting shot at was enough to terrify anyone, but he sensed there was more going on here. He had a sudden image of the older man he'd seen her with at the gun range. "Have you got a jealous boyfriend?" Or worse, "Are you married?"

"Of course not!"

She wasn't married.

"I have to go inside," she said gripping the dashboard with whitened knuckles. "My...mother will be worried."

"Brie, someone shot at us!"

"I know," she said, obviously shaken. "But it couldn't have been Razz."

Razz? "Do you mean that punk kid who hangs out at the arcade?"

Lightning flashed in the distance.

"That punk *kid* is my age," she said without inflection.

Drew cursed under his breath. "Is he your boyfriend?"

"Razz may be a boy in your eyes, but he's no friend of mine."

Rain drummed against the car. He looked from the bullet hole to where she perched on the edge of the seat, hands defensively crossed over her chest. A horrible thought skated through his mind. He'd been so certain

Leland Manning had fired the shot. But what if it hadn't been meant for him at all?

"Are you in some sort of trouble, Brie?"

A loud rumble of thunder made her start. "Of course not, but you know what this town is like. The gossips will have a field day. A mayoral candidate sitting in a parked car with a local waitress."

She was right. They would.

"Please, I have to go inside," she said quickly before he could ask why that mattered. "I have to make sure my...my mother is all right."

Lightning flared, making her freckles stand out against her pale skin.

"Wait. Why did you mention Razz? Is he hassling you?" She'd been staring at the alley between the buildings as he'd driven up tonight. He'd even wondered then if something had spooked her. "Are you afraid of Razz?"

Quickly, Brie shook her head. "Of course not! I only thought of him because...well, I embarrassed him tonight in front of his friends. But he wouldn't come after me with a gun because of it."

She was hiding something. He could sense it.

"Don't worry, I can handle Razz."

Razz was a petty hood. He wouldn't take well to being embarrassed, but firing a rifle at her would be pretty extreme.

"I only know Razz by reputation."

"Then you know Razz," she said dryly.

The rain showed no sign of slackening. Drew knew it wasn't safe for them to continue sitting there in the car. No matter which of them the shot had been intended for, there was only one course of action. "Fasten your seat belt, Brie, we're going to the police station."

"And tell them what? Someone we didn't see in a car we can't identify drove up behind us and fired into the car? What do you think the police will do about this?"

"They'll investigate for one thing."

As the sky lit again he noticed the tiny lines of strain etched around her eyes and mouth. The rough skin of her hands attested to how hard she worked. Only now did he realize how thin she was beneath that shapeless uniform. Frustration hammered at him, matching the rhythm of the rain.

"I can't believe it was Razz, and Police Chief Redfern will never let his officers question Frederick Thane about a drive-by shooting."

The mayor's name was so unexpected he could only gape at her.

"Are you saying you think the mayor of Moriah's Landing drove up behind us and tried to kill me?" he finally asked incredulously.

"Of course not. He hires people to do his dirty work. You're a threat to him, Drew—not like the others who had the temerity to run against him in the past. I'm pretty sure he hired Razz and his friend Dodie to spread a vicious rumor around town. Razz is saying that you murdered Ursula Manning because you were having an affair with her."

The storm was sweeping farther inland, but the incessant rain continued to batter the roof of the car. The night had taken on a surreal feeling.

"Spreading rumors is a long way from murder." And then it struck him. "Is that why you and Razz had words? Were you defending me?"

She opened the door and stepped from the car before he could stop her this time. Rain plastered her hair to her head and molded the thin cotton uniform to her body.

"Call the police," she said, bending over the open door. "I'm sure they'll do up a nice little report for you, there isn't much else they can do. And if anyone bothers to question Razz, I guarantee you he'll have an airtight alibi with a dozen questionable witnesses." She wiped at the water streaming down her face. "Be careful, Drew. If you're smart, you'll stay away from this part of town from now on."

Brie shut the door and ran across the lawn and up the sagging front steps. Unlocking the door, she slipped inside without looking back. The porch light winked out at once. Lightning starkly outlined the house against the storm-filled sky.

Brianna was afraid.

He stared at the bullet hole. A matching hole was visible in the rear window. A very well-placed shot given the wind and rain conditions. Either a marksman had tried to kill one of them, or it had been an incredibly lucky shot. The smart thing—the only sane thing to do—was to have the police investigate.

Drew made no move to recover his cell phone from the back seat.

He had noticed some of the posted scores at the tournament yesterday. Frederick Thane was an excellent marksman.

PULLING UP TO THE MAIN house at the family compound, Drew tried to figure out why he wasn't sitting at the police station. He let himself inside and headed down the hall to his father's office. The opulent house was as silent as a tomb. He stepped inside the empty office and closed the door behind him.

Had he made a serious mistake tonight?

Wind swept against the house, rattling the bank of windows with a mournful howl. Drew thrust his hands in his pockets and stared out at the night. Not that there was much to see. The compound had been designed with privacy in mind. Thick stands of evergreens sheltered the house and the outbuildings from prying eyes. So did the ivy-covered stone walls that surrounded the patrolled grounds.

Out on the cove, a foghorn emitted its mournful warning.

"Just what I need, more atmosphere."

Moriah's Landing had always offered that. He wondered what his ancestors would make of the town today. Running a hand through his damp hair, he gazed unseeingly around the dark, richly paneled office. There was a musty feel to the room. The scent of old cigar smoke lingered in the dark burgundy carpeting and the expensively upholstered guest chairs.

The room's lamps seemed muted, as if the light cowered from the dark shadows hovering in the corners of the room. Drew knew just how that light felt. In those shadows he could almost feel the eyes of his ancestors watching in judgment to see what he would do next.

He strode to the ornately carved serving table, uncorked the heavy lead crystal decanter and poured himself a snifter of the very expensive brandy his father kept there. He hated brandy, yet it seemed oddly appropriate at the moment. If Brie's assumption was correct, he'd nearly joined his ancestors tonight.

He lifted the glass in mocking salute to the ghosts of the past and swallowed a healthy dose of the thick, syrupy alcohol. Instantly, liquid fire seared a path straight down his throat.

Drew managed not to choke.

There was a delicate knock and Nancy Bell stepped inside the room. Her gaze went straight to the glass in his hand and her worried expression deepened. "Drinking alone?"

"Unless you'd care to join me."

"I don't like brandy."

"Me neither." He set the balloon glass down.

Nancy had opted to stay at the main house rather than one of the guest cottages while she was in town. He'd expected to find her here in the office discussing politics with his grandfather at this hour.

"What's going on, Drew?" Nancy demanded without preamble. "You can't pull scenes like the one in the diner today and expect to win an election. Especially not after what happened at the tournament yesterday. If something in your past is coming out to bite us, I need to know about it now."

Nancy glided forward, letting her soft fingers linger against his skin in subtle invitation. Her perfume mingled with the scent of brandy.

"Someone shot a hole through the family sedan tonight."

"What?" She dropped her hand.

Without embellishment, Drew told her everything, including his earlier encounter with Manning, and his suspicion that the scientist had shot at him to get even for his wife's death. Nancy heard him out in silence, though her body tightened at the mention of Brie's name.

"I know you often work with an investigator, Nancy. Do you think he can find out where Frederick Thane was tonight without raising eyebrows or stirring a lot of talk?"

"You can't believe he was responsible. This is incredible."

Nancy paced the room. Drew thought she looked perfectly at home in his father's study. Stylishly elegant, without a hair out of place, he could all but hear her mind whirring as it sorted actions and ramifications.

"I don't understand why you didn't call the police."

Drew wasn't entirely sure why he hadn't either. His stomach contracted every time he thought about how close the shot had come. "Because we didn't see the person or even the car well enough to identify it so there wasn't much point. It's a situation ripe for public speculation."

"Yes. It is. Thane has been mayor a long time. My team learned a few disturbing things during the preliminary investigation, but we couldn't find proof of illegal activities." She paced rapidly, frowning. "You should have called the police. On the other hand, if the shot was intended for the waitress—"

"Her name's Brianna," he said sharply. "She's a friend of mine who just happens to be a waitress." Drew remembered Brie's words. *How do you think it will look? A mayoral candidate, sitting in a parked car with a local waitress.*

Nancy ignored his rebuke. "We definitely don't want to stir up a lot of negative talk around town, which this would definitely do. I'll put some people on Thane and this Razz." She came to a halt in front of him. "Do we have a real name for him?"

"His last name is Razmuesson. I'm not sure about his first name."

"I'll find out."

Nancy laid her hand on his bare arm. Drew couldn't

help but contrast its softness to Brie's work-roughened skin.

"The theory that Thane tried to kill you makes little sense. Manning is a possibility, given his verbal threat, but I'm more inclined to think your *friend* was the intended target. Carey told me you haven't seen her in years. Who knows what she may be involved in?"

Drew wanted to defend Brie, but hadn't he had similar thoughts all the way back to the compound?

"I'll put the investigators on Brianne Dudley and Leland Manning as well. We'll see what turns up."

Drew hesitated. His first instinct was to protest an invasion of Brie's privacy. Only, if she was in trouble, maybe there was some way he could help.

"The police called while you were out," she added with a frown. "They want to talk to you again."

"Was it Cullen Ryan?"

"Yes."

"Okay. I'll call him back in the morning."

"We need to hire a bodyguard for you."

"No bodyguards!"

"But—"

"Nancy, either you're working for my father and my grandfather or you're working for me. You need to decide."

Her hand lingered against his skin. As she gazed at him earnestly, he couldn't miss the subtle invitation in her eyes. Poised, confident, experienced, Nancy was as intelligent as she was attractive.

"I work for you, Andrew. I made that decision when I told you I'd take the job. Your father has an excellent campaign manager of his own, and your grandfather doesn't need one anymore."

"Then I'll go back to my place and get to work on that speech you want me to make."

"Would you like me to…help?"

Looking at her perfect creamy skin, he found himself missing a spray of freckles and bright green eyes.

"Thanks, but I need to do some thinking tonight."

A bit wistfully, the hand dropped from his arm.

"If you change your mind…"

"Thanks, Nancy."

He watched the subtle sway of her hips as she left, closing the door behind her. Nancy Bell was a class act. A man could do a lot worse than have a woman like her for a partner. As long as the man didn't lose sight of the fact that she had an agenda of her own.

"Everyone has an agenda," he told the shadows. The windows rattled in answer.

The Pierce family agenda had always been law and politics and science. Anton Pierce had been a savvy lawyer as well as a respected politician. His wife's family fortune had added a great deal to the Pierce family coffers. Ever since Drew could remember it had been drummed into him that a politician needed the perfect wife.

"Sow your oats while you can, boy," his grandfather had told him the summer after Tasha died. "But you be careful around doxies like that one down at the wharf you've been sniffing after. Use common sense. There must be no scandal to mar our family name. The public is sick and tired of political scandal."

"Brie is hardly a doxie," he'd said, bristling, trying to hide his surprise that the old man knew of his interest in young Brianna Dudley. "She attends Heathrow College, you know."

"On a full scholarship," the old man had said dismissively. "She has no money, no name, no clout, no connections. The woman you select for a wife must be a perfect fit. Can you honestly see that redheaded hoyden sitting down to dinner with the governor?"

The image had brought a smile to his lips then, even as the memory did now. Brianna Dudley didn't have a conservative bone in her body. But when she smiled at Drew with that open, innocent smile, he stopped thinking past tasting those tempting lips.

A tap on the office door brought him back to reality. Zach cracked the door open and stuck his head inside.

"You busy?"

"I'm supposed to be working on my speech. Come on in."

Zach skidded to a halt when he spied the brandy snifter. "I thought you hated brandy. What next? Cigars with the good old boys?"

"Stick a sock in it, Zach."

"What did Ms. Perfect say to upset you now?"

Drew set down his glass and studied his younger brother. There was an edginess to his voice that belied his casual slouch. "Nancy didn't upset me. We were talking strategy."

"Yours or hers?"

Surprised by the astute question, Drew cocked his head. "Is there a point to this conversation?"

His brother slumped against the bookcase. "I need some advice."

"From me?" He kept the surprise out of his voice.

"Even you get some things right."

"Like what?" Drew asked suspiciously.

"Women."

Drew forgot to inhale.

"You've got a reputation."

Embarrassed, he forced himself not to look away. "It's highly exaggerated."

"Hey, this is me, remember? I don't just read the paper. Last year there was the fashion model, then that actress, and—"

"Knock it off. They were just women I dated."

"Exactly. You must use a scorecard to keep track."

"What's your point, Zach?"

"You've dated at least a dozen women in the past couple of years and you've managed to remain friends with all of them."

Except for one redheaded hoyden.

"So I want some advice."

"You want to break up with someone without hurting her feelings?"

"No! You didn't marry any of these women despite the pressure coming from Dad and Grandpa and everyone." Zach rushed as if he had to get the words out quickly. "How did you know none of them were the right woman?"

A sinking feeling settled over him. Drew tried for a light approach. "You thinking of getting married?"

"Maybe."

He ran a hand over his jaw. "You're serious."

"About Emily, I think I am."

"Emily? You don't mean Emily Ridgemont, do you?" Emily Ridgemont was Kat Ridgemont's younger half sister. Kat had been part of the group their sister used to run around with. The last he'd heard, Kat was working as a private investigator with an office down by the wharf. He didn't know anything about her kid sister, though he'd heard some rumors that she had a crush on his brother. Drew hadn't paid any attention at the time.

"I thought you had more sense."

Zach flushed. "She's special, Drew."

Drew shook his head. "She's a kid, Zach. She can't be more than what—sixteen?"

"Seventeen. Almost eighteen. And she's very mature for her age."

"She's jailbait, Zach! If Dad finds out…"

"He won't. And even if he does, I don't care. I'm not the one being groomed to be president of the United States."

Drew sucked in a breath. He regarded Zach with fresh eyes. At twenty, his brother's boyish good looks were firming, taking on the more defined features that come with maturity.

"Want to trade places?" Drew asked softly.

Zach's gaze shifted away. "What I want is to protect Emily. I like her, Drew. I really like her. When we're together, I feel—I don't know, different. When we're apart I can't stop thinking about being with her. Wait until you meet her. She isn't like anyone else. I don't even notice other women anymore."

Drew winced. More than anything, he wished this conversation wasn't taking place. He felt singularly unequipped to handle a discussion on his brother's love life.

"What should I do?" Zach asked earnestly.

Drew exhaled. "Take it slow."

Zach scowled.

"Hey, you wanted my advice. For what it's worth, I'd go slow. Some women want lavish presents and expensive—"

"Em isn't like that."

Once again Drew recognized the man Zach was becoming. It was like looking through a mirror at his own past. For just an instant he was jealous of the world of opportunities his brother had yet to explore.

"Never mind," Zach said, coming away from the bookcase. "Forget I mentioned it. You don't understand."

"You're dead wrong."

Zach stopped walking.

"I know exactly how you feel."

"Yeah, right. That's why you keep a harem."

"Harems are too much work. But there's safety in numbers."

"Yeah? So who was she? The woman that sent you running for safety. This is a whole new side to you. What happened? Dad or Grandpa scare her off?"

Drew's breath suddenly caught in his chest. Why had he never considered that possibility? Because surely Brie would have come to him.

"Oh, man. Is that what happened?" Zach asked.

"No." Brie wouldn't run from a fight, nor would she scare easily. But four years ago she'd still been pretty young. Almost as young as Emily Ridgemont.

"I can just see the old man now shelling out a bundle to pay her off. Emily would never dump me for money."

A hollow feeling opened in the pit of his stomach.

"That isn't what happened." It couldn't have been. He hadn't needed his grandfather's help. "I destroyed the relationship all by myself. I got blitzed one night and…" He hesitated, not wanting to admit what he'd done. But if it would save his brother from making the same mistake. "I destroyed something special."

Zach stared at him.

"If I'd gone a little slower, given her more time…" He shrugged.

"More time for what?"

The memory was a bitter weight on his soul. "To grow up."

Zach blinked. "Man, she really ripped you, didn't she?"

Drew shifted uncomfortably. "Forget it. Next time you want advice, write to one of those columnists in the newspaper."

For a moment, they regarded each other in mutual embarrassment. "Slow, huh?" Zach said finally.

Drew shrugged. "While you're a man—"

Zach's eyes widened.

"—seventeen's really young, Zach. If what you're feeling is real, it will wait—and so will she."

Zach pursed his lips thoughtfully. "So I shouldn't overwhelm her."

"Exactly."

Zach reached for the door handle. "Thanks."

Drew sank back, feeling oddly depleted as his brother left. He stared at the ornately carved wood, alone with the shadows of his troubled thoughts.

He'd taken something precious from the young girl Brie had been. Could he give something back to the woman she had become?

Drew stalked back to the window. It had stopped raining and a light mist was rolling in over the compound. Clouds circled the moon, making him think of vampires and werewolves. Too many horror movies when he was a kid.

He was about to turn away when something moved in the yard.

Chapter Five

Acting on instinct, Drew reached for the light switch and plunged the room into darkness. Standing to one side of the window, he strained to see.

Hunched over, someone crept up the twisty garden path. Drew realized whoever it was would pass close to his window, so he waited.

The figure kept looking toward the house, watching the windows. Remembering the bullet hole through his windshield, he thought about the gun his father kept here in the safe. But Drew had had enough of guns. He wanted answers, not another dead body.

Pausing a few yards from where Drew stood, the person stared up at the window over Drew's head. His parents' bedroom! A faint curl of light from that room reached the man's features. Some of the tension drained from Drew's body. Geoffrey Pierce nodded to himself, straightened and set off again more briskly.

His uncle had his own place near Drew's. A bitter man who felt the scientific community overlooked his accomplishments, Uncle Geoff claimed he was working on a project that would finally get him the scientific acclaim he felt was his due.

Drew had been hearing vague rumors. Now, watching

his uncle prowl the grounds in such a secretive manner, Drew knew it was time to pay attention. The last thing any of them needed was a scandal in an election year.

Drew wasn't overly fond of his father's brother, anyhow. Geoffrey Pierce was a strange man. Tall and slender with thinning blond hair, he was handsome like all the Pierces. Only there was a cruel set to Uncle Geoff's lips and an intensity to his stare that made him manage to look both sinister and weak.

He'd been working closely with Leland Manning recently. Drew knew both men were members of a secret scientific society, but the existence of the organization was an open secret around town. No one had thought anything about it until the FBI began an investigation into members of the group.

Now he wondered about his uncle as the man scurried off, swallowed up by the mist.

DREW'S MOUTH WAS DOING incredible things to hers. His hands held her, stroking gently. She could die from the sensations alone. He made her want with intense yearning. She uttered a tiny sound of demand. Her body sang with need.

Only there were voices nearby. Someone was cutting the grass, coming closer and closer. They'd be discovered if they didn't stop. But she didn't want him to stop. She wanted him to be part of her as they were meant to be.

The sound of the lawn mower bumping the wall below her bedroom window brought Brie bolt upright on the bed. Sunshine and stifling heat filled her room despite the fan she'd left running all night. She struggled to sort dream from reality.

Drew had been making love to her. She'd lived that

dream before. But someone really was mowing the lawn. Her lawn!

Her mother shouldn't be out there cutting the grass!

Tossing aside the badly crumpled sheet, Brie ran to the open window to peer through the screen.

Her mother wasn't mowing the lawn.

Andrew Pierce pushed a shiny wide mower against the edge of the house.

Impossible. Brie wondered if she were still dreaming. He certainly looked like a fantasy. Dressed in a pair of worn jeans and a trim, fitted white shirt with an open V-neck collar Drew could have stepped from her dream. His lightly tanned skin glistened in the hot, humid air. Muscles rippled as he worked.

He was breathtakingly gorgeous.

Drew paused and raised his head, looking directly up at her window. Brie inhaled sharply. He couldn't possibly see her through the screen. Could he? His features were partially hidden beneath a baseball cap and a pair of wraparound sunglasses. He gave her a heart-stopping smile and waved cheerfully.

"Oh, my God." He had seen her!

Nicole!

Brie dashed for the bedroom door. Her daughter's room stood open and empty. So did her mother's room.

"Mom! Mom!" Brie yelled as she flew down the stairs, nearly falling over Max in her panic. Her poor little feline skittered quickly out of her path, racing along in her wake at this new and puzzling game.

Her mother's pet cockatoo, Fitzwiggy, spread his snowy white wings in a flutter of panic as Brie burst into the kitchen.

"Where's the fire? Where's the fire?"

Fitzwiggy had picked up several of her mother's favorite expressions and he sounded hauntingly human when he spoke. Max walked over to give him a perfunctory hiss. Brie ignored them. Where was her daughter?

"Mom?" But she knew the house was empty. There were voices outside. What was going on?

"Hello. Hello. Hello."

"Be quiet, Fitz."

As if agreeing, Max turned with feline dignity to pointedly ignore his nemesis.

"Bad cat," Fitzwiggy told him. "Bad cat."

Bad Cat sauntered over to investigate his food bowl. His action pulled Brie's gaze to a note propped conspicuously against the teapot on the counter over the food dish.

The sight of her mother's clear handwriting calmed her fears even before she started reading.

Mary Jackson and I took the children to the beach for the afternoon. I turned off your alarm so you could sleep in. You've been working too hard, darling. Don't be annoyed. We'll be back before you go to work.

Love, Mom

Brie leaned against the counter in relief. Her daughter was safe. She wasn't even here.

The kitchen clock read eleven-thirty. How could it possibly be eleven-thirty? She hadn't slept much last night, but she was always out of bed by eight. Always. She must still be dreaming. Andrew Pierce could not be in her yard mowing the lawn.

The back door swung open. Brie grabbed the closest item at hand. Andrew Pierce strolled inside as if he'd been doing so for years. He stopped abruptly, looking surprised to see her standing there in her own kitchen.

"Well, good morning, sleepyhead. Planning to make tea or throw that pot at me?"

His lazy perusal flooded her with heat.

"Hello. Hello. Hello."

Drew removed his sunglasses and set them on the table. He wasn't the least bit startled by the bird's greeting. Fitzwiggy fluttered his wings in a bid for attention.

"Hello," he chirped. "Hello."

"Hello again, Fitzwiggy."

Drew knew the name of her mother's bird?

Max stopped crunching. He walked over and began rubbing against Drew's pant legs. He too acted as if Drew's presence was an accepted, everyday occurrence.

"Hey there, Max." Drew bent to stroke her cat. He arched his traitorous back in feline pleasure.

"Again?" Her voice came out rusty, like it often did when she'd just rolled out of bed.

"Sure. We met this morning."

"You…" Had he seen Nicole? No, he couldn't have. He wasn't acting like a man who had just met his daughter. Nicole must have gone down the street to Mary's house to wait for her grandmother before Drew had arrived. "What are you doing here?"

Her pulse stuttered, then raced into overdrive as Drew slowly swept her from head to toe with a gaze of masculine appreciation. His impossibly blue eyes shuttered with a slumberous look of desire. She couldn't seem to catch her breath.

"I'm mowing the lawn," he said softly.

"I know that."

Drew smiled, a slow, sensual smile. Brie could barely hear over the thrumming of her heart.

"Did I wake you? I had no idea you liked to sleep until noon."

"I don't. And it isn't noon yet," she said defensively. She could feel the heat scalding her cheeks. "What are you *doing* here?"

"You mean right here, inside your house? It's okay, you know." His rumbly voice lowered even further, conspiratorially. "Your mother told me to walk in and help myself—"

Her brain stopped functioning. Fantasies, memories, erotic dreams all flooded into her awareness in a rush.

"—to the pitcher of lemonade she left for me." He added the last with a boyish grin, as if he knew exactly where her thoughts had gone spinning.

Mother. The word finally penetrated the sensual haze suffocating her usually rational thoughts.

"You talked to my mother?" The question came out just short of a screech. Fitzwiggy squawked in response. He flapped his wings in an impressive display.

"Easy, Fitz," Drew told the bird calmly. "She's just a little befuddled this morning. Right, Max?"

Max gazed at him inquiringly, then returned to his food dish. Belatedly, Brie set the teapot down before she succumbed to an impulse to hurl it at his head.

"I was worried about you. I wanted to make sure you and your mother were all right after what happened last night."

"You didn't tell my mother someone shot at us?" She could hear the hysterical note creeping into her voice, and from his concerned expression, so could Drew.

"No, I assumed you'd done that. She was on her way out when I got here, so we didn't have a chance to do much talking."

Thank God!

"But that doesn't mean *we* aren't going to talk about it."

The amount of adrenaline pumping through her body couldn't possibly be a good thing, Brie decided. She'd have a heart attack, right here on the kitchen floor.

"You aren't a morning person, are you?" Drew asked as he sauntered over to the correct cupboard without hesitation. Withdrawing a glass he turned to her, a smile hovering at the corners of his mouth. A smile that slowly faded as his gaze skimmed her body. Brie realized she was standing in front of him in only an oversized T-shirt and a pair of skimpy panties.

He set the empty glass on the table beside his sunglasses and removed his baseball cap, running his fingers through his damp hair.

Stress had finally caught up to her. How could such a simple action look like an invitation to sex? She'd lost her mind entirely. Her imagination had gone so haywire he appeared to be looking at her the way she'd wanted him to look at her all those years ago. Covetously. The way she looked at a fresh-baked batch of her mother's cookies.

"I'm not a cookie."

His throaty chuckle traveled right down her spine. "Ah, Brie." He smiled as if he knew exactly what she meant. "As I recall, you taste a whole lot better than any cookie."

He closed the distance between them, stoking the fire of curling desire building low in her belly.

If he touched her, she would dissolve.

If he didn't, she would die.

He reached out. The room receded. Lightly, almost

reverently, he threaded his fingers in her tangled mop of hair.

"You have no idea how sexy you look right now, do you?"

Mutely, she stared at him.

"You're practically eating me alive with that look, Brie. Do you know I used to dream about seeing your hair unpinned and wild?" he said thickly. "Exactly like this."

She...could...not...breathe.

Every sense was heightened. Drew smelled of sweat and cologne, of freshly mowed grass and sunscreen lotion. How could such a combination be so unbearably stimulating? She wanted to lay her hand against his warm skin. She wanted to explore those hard, flat planes.

"I didn't realize your hair would feel this soft," he whispered wonderingly. "Like a river of silken flames."

Oh, God.

The prayer came from her soul—a whispered plea for help. Only Brianna wasn't sure if she was praying to wake up, or praying this wasn't a dream.

"I promised myself I wouldn't do this," he growled huskily.

The kiss started out as soft as a sigh, as potent as an explosion. Every nerve in her body short-circuited. His mouth moved with slow deliberation, tasting, sampling, savoring. The kiss lasted forever, over in the blink of an eye. She parted her lips, staring at him helplessly. He smiled and lowered his mouth to hers once more. He probed the hot, moist cavern of her mouth with his tongue.

Dream and reality merged. This was what she had

been waiting for. The kiss went hot and wild from one beat of her heart to another.

Drew groaned against her mouth. She whimpered in need.

"What are you doing to me?" he whispered, planting tiny kisses along the line of her jaw. "You could tempt a saint to turn in his halo."

"You aren't a saint," she whispered back shakily.

"Definitely not."

He slipped his hands beneath her curls, cupping the back of her head firmly. She was captive to that touch. The sensation was highly erotic. Brie strained against him, wanting more as his mouth worked incredible magic, kissing the curve of her cheek, nibbling her chin, biting lightly at the lobe of her ear. Her legs turned to liquid. As if sensing this, he began to lift her.

"Drew? Hey, Drew. Where the heck are you?"

They sprang apart like guilty children at the sound of Zachary's voice. Drew's brother stood outside the open kitchen window only a few feet away.

Breathing as if she'd run three miles, Brie gripped the counter for support.

Drew muttered fiercely under his breath. He ran a hand through his hair, across his jaw. She was glad to see the slight tremor of his hand. It was a relief to know he wasn't any steadier than she felt.

"Zach has lousy timing."

Or was it good timing? She couldn't seem to think.

"Better put some clothes on," he told her gruffly, but softly so his voice wouldn't carry outside.

Her face flamed. She was a fool.

"Hey, Zach, where's Drew?"

Carey's voice.

"I don't know. He was mowing the lawn a second ago...."

The voices trailed off as the men headed around to the front of the house.

"What did you do, bring a committee?" she demanded.

His shoulders rose and fell. "It was Nancy's idea."

"She's here, too?" An image of the classy, dark-haired beauty was instantly deflating.

"There's quite a few people here. You'd better get dressed."

Oddly reassured by his hungry gaze, she found new courage, born of frustration. "Why? Don't you like my T-shirt?"

His eyes went molten. "Little fox," he whispered. "I love your T-shirt. I may have it bronzed. Now, go take it off."

Her hands shook, but she reached for the hem and began to edge it upward.

"You wouldn't dare."

The smoky flare of his eyes was all the encouragement she needed. Brianna pulled the T-shirt over her head without allowing herself to think about what she was doing. Tossing it at him, she covered her breasts with her arms.

"Call it a souvenir. I'm going up to take a shower." An ice shower—maybe in Alaska.

Brie fled. The last time she'd run from Drew, he'd followed. This time, there was no sound of pursuit. She wasn't sure if she was relieved or sorry as she leaned against the bathroom door, shaking at her temerity.

What had she done?

She knew the why. The same stupid reason she'd made love with him four years ago. It was pitiful. She was pitiful. But she was still in love with Andrew Pierce.

Hadn't she learned anything in all these years? She had just played a fool's game with an expert in the field. The outcome had only one inevitable conclusion.

And this time the stakes were higher. Dangerously higher.

She finally managed to shower and dress and went back downstairs after coming to a decision. She would not give in to the temptation to seduce those indecently sexy jeans right off his body no matter how much she wanted him. She would tell Drew to go away and stay away. She had no place in his life. His grandfather had made her see that without saying a word.

She clung to the memory of the sheer opulence of the Pierce mansion. The rich, dark woods, the ornate paintings, the thick carpeting, the sunken marbled foyer with that grand staircase… Brie gazed at the familiar threadbare carpeting, the old, worn furniture of her childhood. Sly, crafty politician that he was, Anton Pierce had invited her to the family compound with his irresistible offer of help four years ago.

Drew had gone back to school and when her mother needed surgery, she hadn't known where to turn. There was no money, no way out. So she'd accepted Anton Pierce's offer to meet with him, and discuss the situation. Without saying a word, he allowed her see for herself that the differences between them were insurmountable. The old man made it perfectly clear she could never be a part of their world. She'd understood that by taking the money she was agreeing to sever any future relationship with Drew.

Brie closed her eyes. Taking a deep breath, she resolutely strode into her mother's kitchen. Drew was gone. A lawn mower growled several houses away. Going to the window, she saw Drew and a dozen other people—including the elegant Nancy Bell—working in Mrs. Freeson's yard. The elderly widow sat on her front porch swing beaming happily.

What was Drew up to?

Beside her mother's note, Drew had propped his own note against the glass he'd taken down earlier. Instead of lemonade, the glass contained water and a single perfect yellow rose.

Tears blurred her vision. He must have cut the rose from Mrs. Freeson's large garden. That didn't dim the beauty of the gesture, but what did he want from her?

Tonight after work, was all his note said. Flipping it over, she found a computer-generated flyer with Drew's photograph. *Andrew Pierce for Mayor* was the caption above the picture. His hands gripped a lawn mower and the caption underneath read, *When Andrew Pierce says he's going to clean up Moriah's Landing, he means exactly that.*

The picture had been taken in front of her house early this morning. One of his people must have designed and printed copies of the flyer this morning.

Brianna sank down on the nearest chair. The emotions churning inside her were nearly as overwhelming as they'd been the day he'd come to apologize after making love to her.

Drew hadn't come here because of her or even because of what had happened last night. He'd come as a part of his campaign. She'd misunderstood and thrown herself at him once again. Mortified, she wondered how she would ever face him again.

NO DAY EVER ZOOMED PAST with such speed. Suddenly the diner was closed and it was time to leave. Drew hadn't come. She lingered inside as long as she dared before heading home, feeling like a total fool.

Yesterday's storms hadn't daunted the heat or the humidity, but Brie didn't sense any impending storms tonight. She strode briskly, paying close attention to her surroundings on the empty, narrow street. Even the noise from the bars seemed muted tonight. Suddenly, heavy running footsteps were clearly audible. Brie whirled, hand on her mace.

"Brie! Thank God. I was afraid I'd missed you."

"Drew! You scared me. What are you doing here?"

He wasn't even breathing hard. "Didn't you get my note?"

"Of course I got it."

"But you didn't think I'd come."

She'd dreamed. She'd fantasized, but… "Frankly, no," she said flatly.

He was impeccably dressed. His perfectly tailored shirt and well-pressed dress slacks made her unhappily conscious of her stained, ill-fitting uniform.

"I'm sorry, Brie. I tried, but I couldn't get away any sooner. My grandfather insisted on dinner at the Crow's Nest to discuss the new campaign strategy."

The bar door opened across the street. The person either changed his mind or ducked back inside, because no one came out and the door closed quickly. Drew scowled. "Let's go. I'm walking you home."

Her pulse went into overdrive, but she managed to keep her voice even. "What happened to your car?"

"I left it at the restaurant because I knew you preferred to walk."

And Brie couldn't help thinking that by leaving it

there, no one would notice it in front of her house again tonight.

"We need to talk."

Her stomach lurched when she saw his expression. "Because of last night?"

"Of course because of last night. Just because I didn't report the shooting—"

"You didn't?"

"No," he growled, plainly not happy with the decision. "I'm worried about you."

Brie stared up at him in surprise. She told herself not to read too much into his words. Drew would be concerned over anyone he thought was in trouble. Still, her breathing came more quickly.

"Why are you worried about me?"

"Cullen Ryan is in charge of the investigation into Ursula Manning's death."

"I know," she responded, too puzzled by the abrupt turn in the conversation to pursue her question.

Drew scanned the darkness alertly. He lowered his voice. "Leland Manning is claiming his wife was kidnapped several days ago."

Brie halted. "What?" At his prompting, she resumed walking, but at a much slower pace.

"Apparently, Manning withdrew twenty thousand dollars in cash from his account the day before the tournament. Cullen confirmed this. Manning says an anonymous caller told him to leave the money in a hollow stump in the woods the following morning."

"So she was kidnapped?"

No one had been charged with Claire's kidnapping and torture. Now it had happened again? Chills snaked up her spine.

"The medical examiner confirms Ursula had injuries

consistent with being tied up. There were other things that indicated she'd been a hostage. Cullen isn't saying what those other things were.''

Brie shuddered. Claire's body had several unexplained marks and she was severely anemic in addition to being catatonic. Rumors of vampires had abounded. Moriah's Landing loved a good horror story.

''You're thinking of Claire, aren't you?'' Drew asked.

''Yes.''

''So is everyone else.''

''Does Cullen think there is a connection?''

''I don't know, but he can hardly rule it out.''

''There's a rumor that the police don't think the shooting was an accident. Cullen doesn't think you killed Ursula, does he?''

Drew shrugged. ''I don't think so. And I'm fairly sure he doesn't believe I kidnapped and tortured her.''

''Ursula was tortured, too?'' Goose bumps rose along her arms.

''I surmised that from what Cullen isn't saying.''

Drew suddenly stopped moving. He peered around alertly at the dark neighborhood street and the even darker houses.

''What's wrong?''

''I'm not sure. Keep walking. From now on we'll use the car.''

Brie nearly tripped over an uneven spot of pavement. His hand closed over her arm, preventing her from falling.

''You're not planning to make this a habit?''

''Yes.''

For a second, the simple word and his expression

raised impossible hopes. But thinking of her daughter scattered them to oblivion. "You can't."

"Watch me."

She stopped moving. "What do you want from me, Drew? Sex?"

For a timeless second he simply stared at her. "Now, there's a leading question. If I say no, you'll know I'm lying. If I say yes, you'll think that's all I want."

"Isn't it?"

He laid his hand on her arm. "Don't."

"If you dare apologize again, I will not be responsible for my actions." Brie whirled and began walking rapidly. She won the battle, relegating the tears to another place inside her heart. Later, when she was completely alone, she'd give in to them, but she would not cry in front of Drew.

He hurried to catch up. Wisely, he didn't touch her again.

"I seem to spend a lot of time apologizing to you," he said.

"Must be a character flaw."

"Brie, four years ago you were too young for me. We both knew it."

"And now I just live on the wrong side of town?"

Drew swore. "Do you honestly think I care about that? Did Tasha?"

Brie paused once more. "Then I'll repeat the question. What do you want from me?"

"I'd like to be your friend."

"Friend." The word had a bitter taste. "So I can join the legion of your other women *friends?*"

He urged her forward. "The gossip factory at work again, right? Let me tell you something, Brie. You are *nothing* like any other woman I have ever known. I almost wish you were. Maybe then I could stop thinking about you. You're like a splinter under my skin, always there.''

"How flattering." But in a peculiar way, it was.

Lightly, he trailed his hand down her bare arm. The slight caress bumped her heart.

"Don't put up barriers, Brie."

"They already exist. We both know it."

Brie walked more quickly toward her mother's house. In the dark, with its freshly manicured lawn and shrubs, the front steps and railing repaired, the house looked like any other along the street. Only the absent hum of an air conditioner and the open windows set it apart.

"Thank you for mowing the lawn and fixing things today. I appreciate it, even if it was part of your campaign strategy."

"It was the only way I could think of to see you without raising gossip. Of course, I never expected to see quite so much of you, but I'm not complaining."

She was glad he couldn't see the color of her face. "I thought you said it was Nancy Bell's idea."

"It was," he admitted honestly. "You should know I told her what happened last night."

Brie tensed.

"She came up with the campaign slogan to reduce gossip while doing some real good in the community. Maybe we'll even generate a few votes. And I like helping people, making a difference. I know that sounds trite—"

"No. Helping people is never trite. Your empathy is one of the reasons you'll make a great politician."

"Thanks. Want to join my campaign? We're working on the float tomorrow. You could come and help."

Her heart fluttered. She longed to say yes. "I can't. I'm attending a lecture at the college tomorrow."

"You're still going to school?"

Dangerous ground. She shouldn't have mentioned the class. "Dr. Manning is giving a lecture on genetic research that I'm interested in hearing. It's rare to see Manning outside his laboratory, so I'm very eager to attend."

Drew tensed. "He's giving a lecture tomorrow? With his wife still in the morgue?"

"I know. I expected his talk to be rescheduled, but I understand Dr. Manning told the college he needs to work in order to get past his grief."

While she shared Drew's skepticism, everyone in town knew Manning was strange.

"Planning to be one of his test subjects to see if you are really a witch?" Drew asked.

"Oh, I already know that. My mother's line is descended from one of the witches they hung here in Moriah's Landing."

"Really? That explains it, then."

She faced him, feeling her heart pound. He was going to kiss her again. And God help her, she was going to let him.

"You've bewitched me, Brie. Ever since the night of that party, I've been under your spell."

She trembled, even as she melted into his arms. Hungrily, his lips closed over hers. Without warning, light pinned them in a beam so bright, she was blinded.

Chapter Six

Drew shoved her behind him as another flash went off. He started toward the car and the searchlight winked off. Helplessly, he watched the car race out of sight. A dog was barking angrily.

Brie had made him forget everything, including caution. If the passenger had had a gun instead of a camera, they'd both be dead right now.

"Did you see who it was?"

"I saw. Razz."

She inhaled sharply. One of her elderly neighbors and his dog hurried over to them.

"You folks okay?"

"Yes, sir. Thank you."

"Blasted hooligans and their pranks," the old man said. "The police oughta do something about these kids before they give someone a heart attack."

Drew knew exactly what he wanted to do to Razz.

"You're the Pierce boy, aren't you? Didn't recognize you right off. My eyesight isn't too good anymore. That was a nice thing you did today. Everybody's talking about how you were out here working to help the neighborhood. A'course now I see you had an ulterior motive," he added with a chuckle. "Don't blame you one bit. Our Brie here's a lovely girl. Lovely."

Behind them, the front door opened. A dim figure stepped onto the porch. "My mother," Drew heard Brie whisper.

"Go inside, Brie, I'll talk to you tomorrow."

He expected an argument, but she only hesitated a second before nodding.

"Good night, Drew, Mr. Lee."

Drew watched her run lightly up the steps to her mother. He waved, forcing down the adrenaline that insisted he go chasing after Razz and that camera immediately. First he needed to be sure everyone got safely back inside.

"Such a nice family," Mr. Lee was saying. Brie and her mother disappeared inside the house. "Shame about Pamela's cancer returning."

"Pamela Dudley has cancer?" Pieces of the puzzle clicked into place.

"Sure. I'm not tellin' tales out of school since she never made a secret of it. As soon as brain cancer was diagnosed four years ago, I told my Alice it would take a miracle. Had a cousin died of brain cancer. They didn't get all his tumor, either. Damn shame. It's so unfair. With the little girl and all, I don't know what young Brie's going to do."

"Albert?" A woman's voice called out stridently. "Albert!" The dog began pulling at the leash to go back home.

"Busted," the old man said with a cheerful grin. "I was hoping she wouldn't notice I forgot to take the garbage out again. Nice talkin' with you, son."

Questions filled Drew, but Albert Lee and his dog

were moving spryly across the lawn. Besides, Drew realized the answers he wanted should come from Brie.

Why hadn't she told him? Didn't she know she could
come to him for help?

Of course not. How would she know that? Four years
ago he took her innocence and walked away. In her
place, he wouldn't trust him, either.

The front of her house was dark already, the door
shut tight. His questions would wait until morning. He
had a wise-mouthed punk and a camera to find. Brie
wasn't going to be the source of any gossip if he could
help it. What a stupid night to have left his car and his
cell phone so far away. As he jogged down the street
he wondered if he could pull Carey away from his latest
woman long enough to help him search for Razz.

"WHAT WAS DREW DOING BACK here at this hour?"
Pamela Dudley asked. "And what was that bright light
I saw?"

"Kids were playing a prank with a car spotlight."
Brie didn't add that someone had taken their picture.
Fear sat like a lead weight in her belly.

She lifted Max, who had come running across the
kitchen to greet her. His long silver tail swished impa-
tiently and he mewed in irritation. The source of his
displeasure, a tiny kitten, opened sleepy gold eyes and
blinked curiously at her from its curled position against
her daughter's sleeping form.

Brianna came to an abrupt halt. "What on earth?"

"I'm afraid your daughter's familiar showed up in
the backyard today."

"Very funny."

The kitten was a tiny puffball of long, mostly white
fur. A calico, it had a comical, pointed face that stared

at Brianna curiously, blinked at Max, then dismissed them both with typical feline indifference. The kitten settled herself more snugly against Nicole.

"We can't keep her, Mom."

"Fitzwiggy and Max agree with you, but I'm afraid Nicole and Little Imp have a different take on things."

"You've named her?"

"Actually, Nicole named her."

"Oh, Mom, a tiny kitten like that probably already has an owner. She looks part Persian or something."

"She's something, all right," her mother told her wryly. "Hence the name—unless you'd prefer 'Bad Cat' like Fitz does. She wandered up to your daughter when the children were playing in the backyard. I asked around, Brie, but no one seems to know where she came from."

"The last thing we need is another animal. Why didn't you tell Nicole no?"

Her mother smiled. "For the same reason you won't. After all, we're supposed to be descended from witches," her mother teased affectionately. "All good witches have familiars."

"Uh-huh. And magical powers, too, but I've never met a broomstick I could make fly."

Her mother laughed softly. "You used to have a lot of fun trying."

Brie ignored that rejoinder. "Who ever heard of a witch with a cockatoo for a familiar?" she scoffed, nodding toward the birdcage in the corner.

Her mother smiled. They both knew Brie was going to lose this battle. There was so little she could give her daughter. And the kitten was adorable. It had a black-and-brown patch over its left eye that lent it a cocky, defiant sort of look. Little Imp might be small, but she looked like she'd challenge the world if she had to.

Her mother went over and fussed with Fitzwiggy, offering him a treat before sliding the cover over the large cage for the night. "You never did say what Drew was doing here tonight."

Brie tensed. "You two must have gotten pretty chummy this morning if you're on a first-name basis."

"He reminds me of his sister, Tasha. He seems very nice, Brie."

"He's running for mayor, Mom. He has to be nice."

"Does he know about his daughter?"

The room spun. Brie forgot to breathe.

"Hard to miss those eyes, dear. You never told him, did you? I wondered when you suddenly started dating all those boys that fall. You didn't want anyone to know who her father was, did you?"

"No." It came out a croak.

"Why not?"

"I made a promise."

Her mother studied her expression. She seemed to age right before Brie's eyes. Her shoulders sagged. Pain filled her eyes. "So that's it. I always wondered where you got the money for my surgery. Maureen paid you off, didn't she."

"Drew's mother? No. She doesn't know. No one knows. I got the money from Drew's grandfather. He didn't want me seeing Drew anymore. Not that he said that. He was too smart to issue edicts. He offered me money instead. To help out, as he put it. Then he talked about Drew's career."

"Oh, Brie…"

"I didn't know about the baby then. We needed the money and Drew had already made it clear he regretted what happened, so I promised his grandfather I wouldn't see Drew again. I didn't think it would be a problem. Drew had gone back to school. Our...relationship was just one of those things.''

''You should have told me.''

''What could you have done?''

''But when you found out about Nicole—''

''You'd started your treatments. They were scheduling the surgery.''

''You shouldn't have taken the money, Brie. We'd have managed somehow.''

''I didn't *take* the money, Mom. I borrowed it. I've been paying Mr. Pierce back a little out of each paycheck ever since.''

A tear slid silently down her mother's cheek. ''I'm sorry, Brie. So sorry.''

''You have nothing to be sorry for. If you hadn't been ill, the results would have been the same except that I wouldn't have taken any money. It all worked out.''

''Did it?''

Her mother looked toward the sleeping child. ''How long do you think you can keep Nicole a secret? Drew is bound to realize the truth as soon as he sees her.''

''We won't let him see her!''

''Oh, Brie. Do you think that's fair? Don't you think he would want to know his daughter?''

Her heart filled with anguish. ''Think about Drew, Mom. What would it do to his campaign chances, if word got out I'd had his baby and he calmly went on with his life? You know how funny people are around here. If they learn he had an affair with a waitress—''

''Oh, Brie. You're in love with him, aren't you? You were infatuated with him even when you were young.''

''Don't worry, I'm completely over any infatuation.''

Her mother glanced pointedly at the yellow rose now sitting in her cut glass bud vase in the kitchen window. "But is he over you?"

FREDERICK THANE WIPED at the sweat trickling down the side of his face. He hated the heat and he hated meeting in the dead of night like this. He wanted to be back inside his air-conditioned house, in the comfort of his king-sized waterbed.

How could it still be so hot out here in the middle of the night? Moriah's Landing was a beach town.

"I think you'll be more than happy with this," the youth said smugly. "The high and mighty Andrew Pierce is gettin' it on with a waitress from the diner."

How he would have liked to wipe that sneering expression from the boy's face.

"I'm a little worried about that publicist of his. She's got people askin' questions around town."

"Don't worry about Ms. Bell. I'll handle her. She doesn't know anything and she won't. Nothing she can prove."

Razz snorted indignantly. "You don't hafta prove things in an election year. You just gotta convince the public things are true. People aren't so bright, you know. A few whispers, a couple rumors..."

Surprised by this unexpected perception, the mayor glanced around nervously once again at the dark shadows that encompassed them.

"Shut up, you fool," he whispered.

"Who you callin' a fool, old man? I'm safe even if they bring you down."

The mayor ground his teeth. How he hated dealing with this punk. If the kid and his friends weren't so useful...but they were. He would have to put up with a little aggravation and inconvenience from time to time. Like now.

Glancing around once more at the empty pier, he tried to shake off the feeling they were being watched. The hairs on the back of his neck stirred uneasily. His breathing coarsened. He tried to meld even deeper into the shelter of the building beside him.

"No one's bringing me down," he whispered fiercely. "I know where *all* the bodies are buried, understand?" Thane handed the boy a tightly wrapped package, careful not to touch those disgusting hands. "Remember that and keep your mouth shut."

The boy whistled through teeth stained yellow by nicotine. "I always do, don't I?"

Something stirred in the still air. Both men peered around uselessly. There was nothing to see beyond the restless waves lapping at the beach. Yet there was something out there in the night. A feeling. As if the ghosts of Moriah's Landing were stirring just out of sight.

Thane consoled himself with the knowledge he was safe. No one could prove a thing against him. He'd always taken precautions. He would continue to take them. Still, he felt the unseen forces gathering over the town expectantly.

"Let me worry about the details," the boy said arrogantly, startling him from his crazy thoughts. "Everything's set for the Fourth. The mighty Andrew Pierce will wish he'd gone elsewhere to launch his career."

"See that he does."

There was no choice. Thane was not giving up his cushy situation for anyone. Especially not a Pierce. He would do whatever it took, use whoever he needed, to prevent Pierce from succeeding in his quest.

A tiny lick of air sent a chill of apprehension down

his back. Thane turned away sharply and headed back toward his car. He wished he could shake this feeling that something bad was about to happen.

"DODIE AND RAZZ AREN'T hanging around the arcade today, Drew. Nobody's seen them. Carey's still out searching."

Drew finished tying a paper carnation together to attach to the float and nodded. "Thanks for trying, Zach."

"How'd your session go with Cullen Ryan this morning? Did you tell him what happened?"

"No."

Zach frowned. "Did he say if he got the ballistics report yet?"

"No. He's not saying much of anything."

"I got the same sense last night when he talked to me and Nancy. He was especially interested in what we saw before the shooting."

"You mean who."

Zach nodded. Nancy Bell strode around the corner of the float. Volunteers were swarming over it, putting paper carnations in place.

"Hi, Zach. I wondered where you got to this morning. Drew, your grandfather called. He wants to see both of us right away. I gather it's urgent."

"It generally is with my grandfather." But Drew's stomach lurched all the same. An urgent meeting with his grandfather did not bode well.

"Have fun," Zach said.

Drew handed his brother the carnation and indicated the pile of paper still waiting to be folded. "Make yourself useful. We'll be right back."

Drew's gaze narrowed when he and Nancy finally reached the compound and approached the main house down the long, tree-shrouded driveway. His father's distinctive car sat prominently in front of the main house.

"I thought your parents weren't coming home until much later this evening."

"They weren't," he replied flatly. Drew's instincts were on full alert, particularly when his mother met them at the door.

"You're back ahead of schedule," he said, giving her a quick hug.

"Your grandfather called very early this morning. I gather something has happened."

Drew shrugged as she greeted Nancy.

"They're waiting for you two in the office. You'd better hurry along."

Nancy's cell phone rang as they started down the hall. She stopped walking to check the caller ID. "It's my investigator."

"Take the call. I'll tell them you'll be right in."

The darkly paneled room still smelled of cigars and brandy, though neither his father nor his grandfather had either one in evidence. What they did have were matching scowls. His grandfather sat stiffly behind the polished wood desk, tapping an envelope against several sheets of paper. Drew's father paced back and forth in front of the bank of windows.

"Nancy had a phone call," Drew said by way of greeting.

"Explain," Anton Pierce demanded, holding out the top sheet to Drew.

Two pictures, surprisingly clear considering the conditions under which they'd been taken. While the background was dark and indistinct, Drew's features were unmistakable. So were Brie's, especially in the second picture. The first showed them kissing. In the second, the two of them were turning startled faces toward the searchlight. They looked guilty as sin.

"He must have used a digital camera and a high-quality inkjet printer," Drew mused.

"Is that all you have to say?" his father demanded.

Scowling darkly, his grandfather handed him a sheet of paper.

Drew uttered a word he didn't generally use.

"The photographer wants money or he'll release these pictures to the press."

Drew stared into the older man's cold gray eyes. "Tell him to go to hell."

"Of course. That goes without saying. But we'll have to do some damage control. Perhaps Ms. Dudley could be persuaded to leave town for a time. It seems I misjudged her character the last time. I thought when she began paying the money back..."

Something twisted inside him. Drew laid his palms flat on the desk and leaned down. "What money?"

Anton Pierce blinked. "That is not important. What is important—"

"It's important to me," Drew said coldly. "What money?"

"Andrew, don't take that tone with your grandfather," William Pierce scolded.

Drew never lifted his head. "Did you pay Brie off four years ago?"

"Of course I did. You refused to heed my warning. Fortunately, Ms. Dudley was more amenable. She was only too willing to take the money in return for staying away from you," he added harshly.

Drew forced words past the fury choking him as he straightened and faced his relatives. "This isn't the first time you've interfered in my life, but it will be the last."

The room went so still he could hear the soft rattle of his grandfather's breathing.

"You paid the wrong person. You should have tried paying *me* to stay away from *her*." Drew headed for the door before his uncertain temper caused him to say something irrevocable.

"Where are you going?" his father demanded. "We have to decide how to handle this situation."

Drew paused at the heavy oak door. "I know exactly how I'm going to handle this situation. I'm going to warn Brie and apologize again."

"Warn the waitress?" his father sputtered.

"Apologize for what?" his grandfather asked in outrage.

A calm settled over him as he regarded the two men he'd looked up to and respected all his life. Arguing was as pointless as explanations.

"Don't you realize what will happen if the blackmailer takes these pictures to the local rag? You'll be a laughingstock," his grandfather snarled.

"If my reputation can't survive those innocent pictures, then the family name isn't worth much, is it? Make no mistake. I will not have Brie's reputation destroyed by some cheap politician who thinks he can intimidate me."

"You aren't going to accost Thane, are you?" his father demanded.

Thinking about what he'd like to do to Frederick Thane curled his fingers. There was no doubt in his mind that the mayor was behind the pictures and the note. "Not immediately, no. First I'm going to warn Brie. Then I'm going to find Edgar Razmuesson and teach him a few things. *Then* I'll go and have a polite discussion with our sleazy excuse for a mayor. You'd better have Nancy stick around. We may need her services when I'm through.''

''Andrew Pierce, get back here!''

Drew ignored the raised clamor of voices and closed the door. He nodded toward his mother, who stood on the staircase, clutching the polished wood bannister. Nancy was not in sight.

''Andrew?''

''Later, Mom. Tell Dad I borrowed his car.'' He'd driven over in Nancy's car and he was too angry to go looking for her. Still, he didn't really want to leave her without letting her know.

His mother's voice joined the chorus as he left the cool, dark, air-conditioned house and stepped into the heat and humidity outside. As expected, his father had left his keys in the car. Drew started the engine and Nancy came running from the house.

''Drew! Wait!''

He rolled down the passenger window. ''I'll talk to you later, Nancy.''

''But, you need to know what my investigator just told me.''

Drew hesitated. Nancy leaned inside the open window. ''Did you know Brianna Dudley gave birth to a baby girl three years ago?''

Not her sister. Her daughter.

''She listed the father as unknown. Is there any chance the baby was yours?''

Breathing suddenly required concentration. He forced himself to exhale slowly. There was more than a chance. Did his grandfather know? Was that the real reason the old man paid her off?

"You didn't know, did you?"

He felt oddly hollow inside. Anger built slowly, tempered by an odd sense of deflation. "Don't say a word to anyone about this."

"Wait! What are you going to do? I'll go with you."

"No," he said firmly. "I'll call you later."

"Drew, you won't do anything foolish, will you?"

"I already did."

Chapter Seven

The lecture was over her head, but Brie got the gist even though she wasn't a biology student like most of the others in attendance. Hope surfaced. Leland Manning had a possible treatment that could save her mother.

Brie waited while the students flocked to his side afterward asking questions. Coldly aloof, he answered impersonally, almost by rote. The room was nearly empty when a gangly young man with thick glasses approached. He could have come from central casting with the word *nerd* stenciled on his bio.

"Dr. Manning, is it true you really believe that witches with supernatural powers exist?"

Manning fixed him with a penetrating gaze. The youth shifted but held his ground.

"Only a fool scoffs at what he doesn't understand."

"Oh, come on, Doctor. Witches?"

"There are people with powers and abilities science hasn't been able to explain. I believe so-called witches are nothing more than normal people with a gene that has heightened talents we are all born with."

"Like flying on a broomstick?" the youth derided,

pushing at the glasses sliding down the bridge of his nose.

Manning's piercing stare became so intense the boy backed up a step, looking suddenly younger and far less sure of himself than he had just a moment ago.

"There are documented cases of telekinesis. There are documented cases of telepathy. There are documented cases of people seeing into the future."

"Well, yes but—"

"Herbal medicine is making a resurgence in this country. Many skilled physicians are now sending their patients for alternative treatments that would have been considered nothing short of witchcraft in the 1600s."

"Okay, but—"

"Science holds the answers to everything. Sadly, self-proclaimed scientists are just now starting to ask the right questions. Witches and their powers exist, young man. But there is nothing supernatural about those abilities."

Manning's expression darkened. His features took on the look of a true fanatic. His eyes all but glowed. They seemed to bore right through his victim. The boy appeared to shrink right before Brie's eyes.

"One day, we will discover the genes that control these abilities. We will be able to isolate these genes, tap into them and heighten those latent abilities in so-called normal people. When you look past any myth, you find the reality." His body seemed to vibrate with the fervor of his words. He leveled the boy with a look of contempt. "A closed mind is of no value in the scientific community. You are a fool," he pronounced.

Gathering up his notes, Manning strode past the small, shocked remaining audience, leaving the room and the red-faced student behind. Brie hesitated long enough to fortify her courage and push doubts aside before running after him.

"Wow," she heard a boy say, "that's one scary dude."

Brie agreed. Manning was terrifying, but fear was a luxury she couldn't afford. She left the building and went after him. "Dr. Manning? Dr. Manning! May I have a moment of your time?"

Manning pivoted. He glowered at her. Her courage faltered.

"What is it?"

"A-about your research. Into curing cancer?" She would not allow herself to be cowed. Her mother's life was at stake. "When will you be ready to start human testing?"

"Are you volunteering?"

Overhead, the intense sun dimmed as a cloud skipped across its surface. Chills raced down her arms despite the late-afternoon heat. Leland Manning's avid stare made her want to retreat and keep going. Only desperation kept her standing before him.

"No! That is, I don't need gene therapy, but my mother does. She has brain cancer."

"Then I suggest she consult an oncologist."

He started to turn away. She laid a detaining hand on his jacketed arm. She quickly dropped it to her side, startled by the energy inside this man.

"She has seen an oncologist. She's had all the treatments, but the surgery wasn't successful. They weren't able to get all the cells. Her tumor is returning. You're her only hope."

He studied her as if she were a particularly useless stain on a slide under his microscope. How had any woman dared to marry this man?

"Even if I were ready to test my theories, the cost of this sort of therapy is prohibitive. Insurance doesn't cover experimental treatments, you know."

"I do know," she said stubbornly.

He named a sum that made her gasp. With a cold smile of dismissal he turned and began striding away. She couldn't let him do that. There weren't any options. Heart pounding, she played her ace.

"My mother is descended from a local witch."

The doctor stopped walking. He turned slowly. Her heart threatened to burst through her chest as his unwavering gaze cemented her in place.

"Which witch?"

She rolled her hands into fists to keep them from shaking. "Annabel Trantor."

Brianna could practically see him cataloging and sorting through his memory bank for the knowledge marked "Annabel Trantor."

"You are a direct descendant?"

"Yes." Something avaricious in his expression made her want to deny it. "My family lineage is unbroken." She resisted the urge to quail from that expression and slink away.

"Would you be willing to let me have a sample of your blood for my research?"

Her mind recoiled in horror. The oily seduction of that question repulsed her. But as much as she disliked Leland Manning, she would do whatever it took to get help for her mother.

"Yes," she agreed before she could have second thoughts. "Absolutely. But only if you're willing to consider my mother's case."

The smile froze her blood.

"Very well." He named a lower price. "I'll review

her records and let you know my findings. In the meantime, you'll need to find a way to come up with that amount. To cover my cost, you understand.''

"I will.'' Somehow. If it meant selling everything she owned.

"And you understand this is experimental. Your mother could still die. Unless my theory is correct and this protocol works as it should.''

"So there is a chance?''

"A slim chance.''

"We'll take it,'' she said stubbornly.

"Very well. Her name?''

"Pamela Dudley. Sheffield Thornton is her oncologist. He's the one who told me about your research.''

Manning nodded, filing that information away as well. He reached in his pocket to withdraw a leather business card holder. The ivory card was embossed in a dark red that reminded her of blood.

Her hand shook so badly she nearly dropped his card. Everything inside her wanted to cringe away from the aura this man projected.

"Thank you.''

"Perhaps I should be thanking you.'' He inclined his head and strode away. Brie stared after him long after he'd disappeared from sight. The sun slowly crept from behind the cloud as if making certain he was gone first. Its warmth did little to negate the chill that had seeped inside her. No wonder people called Manning a vampire. He had the most terrifying presence she had ever encountered.

She began walking toward the town green to meet her mother and daughter. Her heart was heavy with the weight of fear and worry. She was thankful that at least she didn't have to work tonight.

Had she made a mistake approaching Manning? Would her mother thank her, or reject the idea completely? Brie had known experimental procedures were costly, but how was she ever going to pull together enough money to do this? Even if her mother was willing to use the house as collateral, it wouldn't be nearly enough. Their credit was good, but Brie was a waitress. What bank would take a chance on someone like her?

A silver sedan roared up beside her, honking to gain her attention. She was startled when Drew leaned across the seat and threw open the passenger door.

"Get in."

People were everywhere, but no one seemed to be paying them any attention.

"I can't. I'm meeting my mother at the library."

"I'll give you a lift."

For a moment, she didn't move. His stern expression told her something was very wrong. Brie slid inside.

"How many cars do you own?" she asked nervously when he didn't say anything.

"It's my father's," Drew said tersely.

His fingers gripped the steering wheel like a vise. Fearfully, she searched his features for a clue as to what was wrong. "What is it? What are you doing here? I thought you were working on the float this afternoon."

"I was."

His flat tone alarmed her even more.

"What is it? My…mother?"

"No. Nothing like that. Look, I don't want to have this conversation while I'm driving."

"I don't understand." She took a deep breath as he steered the car toward the town green. "There'll be people all over the park," she reminded him nervously.

"Are you ashamed to be seen with me?"

The darkly asked question bewildered her. "Of course not. I was thinking of you, not me."

Drew pulled into a parking space, killed the engine and stared at her. Busy people were everywhere, setting up for tomorrow's festivities, but he ignored the activity, focusing on Brie.

"Why is it you think I'd be ashamed to be seen with you, Brie?"

Mutely, she stared at him, her eyes wide with apprehension. Drew found he couldn't blurt out the question eating at him.

"Why didn't you come to me when your mother got sick four years ago?"

Color leached from her face. The sprinkle of freckles stood out in harsh contrast.

"Why would I go to you?"

Her genuine puzzlement cut deep. "*I* would have given you the money with no strings attached."

Red suffused her pale cheeks, but she lifted her chin and held his gaze. "But you weren't around anymore, now were you?"

Drew cursed. Brie reached for the door handle before he could stop her. She was halfway to the gazebo before he caught up to her.

"Take your hand off me."

"Calm down." But he released her arm. "We have to talk. I want to know—"

"Mommy, Mommy, Mommy!"

The universe spun and shattered. As if from some enormous distance, Drew watched a miniature version of Brianna break away from Pamela Dudley as they left the library. The child pelted across the grass toward Brie. He didn't need the consternation on Pamela's face, or Brie's stricken expression to know the truth. He saw those same brilliant blue eyes every day when he looked in the mirror.

"There you are. We got a book on kittens, see? Gran'ma says we gotta train Lil' Imp right."

"Grandma's right," Brie whispered. She cleared her throat, hugging the little girl close.

"Too tight, Mommy."

"Sorry, honey." Her voice was shaken. "Where's Imp now?"

"Gran'ma took her to the vet. She's there now. She has to get shots just like me. Do you think Lil' Imp will cry?" the child asked.

"No, sweetie. She'll be brave just like you."

Drew tried to relax his fists, but he doubted anything would unclench the pain gripping his insides. Nancy's investigator had been right. Brianna had had his baby. And she'd never told him. Tears stung his eyes as the enormity of the truth settled over him.

"Who are you?" the little girl asked suddenly, looking up at him.

Your daddy. The words formed in his head, but he couldn't get them past his lips. His daughter. And he hadn't known.

"Do you got a kitty? I do. Her name's Lil' Imp, 'cause Gran'ma says she's a holy terror just like me."

He became aware of Pamela Dudley standing to one side. Lines of strain had etched themselves deeply around her mouth and eyes. Her green eyes, so like her daughter's, observed him from a well of sadness.

"Hello, Drew."

"Mrs. Dudley," he acknowledged. "Brie's daughter was just telling me about her cat."

Pamela flinched but nodded. "Yes. She's pretty excited about having a kitten of her own."

The beautiful child also watched him, as if sensing the tension that isolated the four of them there on the busy green.

"I always wanted a pet," he told his daughter softly, "but my parents wouldn't let me have one."

"Not even a bird?" the child asked.

"Not even a goldfish."

"Gran'ma's got a bird. He's big and white."

"Yes. I've met Fitzwiggy."

Pamela reached for her granddaughter's hand. "Come on, Nicole."

His daughter's name was Nicole. Hurt, regret, anger. So many emotions tumbled inside him that his equilibrium was threatened.

"Let's go get that ice cream now. We have to pick up Little Imp and get her home. I'm sure she's hungry by now."

"Isn't Mommy coming, too?"

"No," Drew stated before Brie could break her silence. "Mommy is going to stay and talk to me for a while. Is that okay?"

The child hesitated. She reached out her tiny hand and touched the back of his. Anger and resentment drained away, leaving only regret. His daughter.

"Okay," Nicole said solemnly. "Bye, Mommy. Bye, man. Come on, Gran'ma."

Brie straightened with a fragile care that was almost painful to watch.

"I couldn't tell you because you weren't here to tell," Brie said quietly.

"What about the day I came to see you at the college? You were laughing with some boy, but you must have known then."

She lifted her chin, her expression blank. "Yes."

"Why didn't you tell me?"

"Does it matter?"

"Yes!" The intensity of his feelings surprised even him. It mattered a great deal. "Was it because of what happened that night? Or because of my grandfather?"

"Your grandfather didn't know, either. No one knew. No one ever would have known if you hadn't come back to town and decided to run for office."

"Brie, those eyes are impossible to miss."

"Not if you had stayed in your part of town. I did what I had to do to survive. And I'll continue doing whatever I need to do to protect my family."

Stunned, he shook his head. "Protect them from what? Me?"

"You, your cold, imperious family, the sly comments of the town—anyone and everyone. Nicole is *my* daughter. It was a one-night stand. You even *apologized!* Or don't *you* remember?"

Her pain lashed him where he stood.

"Get back in your car. Drive back to your safe little compound. We'll forget this scene ever took place."

The last of his anger trickled away as he saw how badly she was trembling. He could almost taste her fear. And that was another lash. Brie was afraid. Of him.

"Nicole is my daughter."

Panic suffused her face. "No! She's *my* daughter! A quickie in a sand dune doesn't make you a father."

She whirled away, but not before he glimpsed the sheen of tears in her eyes. Drew stood there, trying to marshal his chaotic thoughts. He stared up at the gnarled branches of the massive oak tree where they used to hang women branded as witches. He seldom came here. There was a malignant sensation of evil under that dark canopy of leaves. Drew looked to where

Brie stood, a few yards away. Her head was bowed. Was she wiping at tears?

Torn between anger, hurt and sorrow, Drew thrust his hands deep into his pockets and set off in the opposite direction. He wasn't ready for the sort of talk the two of them needed to have. He had some thinking to do first.

BRIE WIPED furiously at her eyes, expecting his hand on her shoulder any second. But the hand never came. When she turned around, Drew was gone.

Stunned, she scanned the park looking for him, but there were too many people. Why had he walked away? What was he thinking? Did he hate her? The thought was unbearable. What was she going to do?

Slowly, she headed for a path that would carry her out of the park. When Drew's green sports car pulled up beside her on the street, her heart began pounding rapidly. But it was Carey, not Drew, behind the wheel.

"Want a lift?"

Brie hesitated, but she wanted to get home and be with her daughter. Accepting his offer would make that happen quicker.

"Thanks. Isn't this Drew's car?" she asked getting in.

"My car's still in the shop. They claim they're having trouble getting the part it needs. Drew lent me this one while I'm waiting."

Brie nodded, but she wondered why Carey hadn't borrowed a car from someone in his own family. The Eldrich clan had nearly as much money as Drew's family did. Brie gave Carey directions and they rode in uncomfortable silence until they pulled onto her street.

"Look," Carey said abruptly. "I don't want to get

into your business, but Drew's my friend. Your association with him...well, it could prove awkward, if you know what I mean.''

Brie had never cared for Carey. He was too vain, too flashy, too arrogant. And he'd had a reputation on campus when she was going to school.

''Awkward how?''

''Uh, well, to put it delicately, you aren't his type.''

''Does Drew know that?''

He reddened. ''Look, Brie, Drew has women falling all over him. You're very attractive, don't get me wrong, but I'm talking gorgeous models, movie stars—''

''Rich people?'' she asked.

''Well, uh, yes.''

''Ah. So you think I'm outclassed in all areas.''

Carey swore. ''Drew'll have my head.''

Brie relented, seeing he was genuinely upset. ''Only if I tell him. Which I won't.''

He pulled to the curb in front of her mother's house. The garage stood open and empty, which meant her mother and daughter weren't home yet.

''Look, just forget I said anything at all, okay?'' Carey asked.

''Carey, I know I'm out of my league.''

''Hey, look, I didn't mean—''

''Of course you did, but it's the simple truth, isn't it? Drew's going to make a terrific mayor, and one day I'm going to be a lawyer. But all we can ever be is friends, so don't worry.''

''Oh. Well. Okay then.'' He studied her openly. A flicker of masculine interest lit his eyes. ''You really are quite attractive, Brie.''

He sounded surprised. Brie didn't know whether to

laugh or be insulted. Carey might be handsome, but he was a rather superficial sort of person.

"You may not have money, but you do have class."

Brie blinked in surprise.

"You should know his family handpicked Nancy Bell to be more than his publicist."

"I figured as much."

"Sometimes Drew chafes under his family yoke, but he generally comes around and does what they want. His folks have been after him since he finished school to get married. And his grandfather's been drilling it into his head for years that he needs the right woman by his side if he's going to run for president one day."

"Like I said, don't worry. I have no aspirations to be the first lady." The very idea was too ludicrous to contemplate. "Thanks for the ride home."

"Sure. My pleasure. Look, uh, Brie, I'm, uh, not planning to run for office. Mind if I stop by the diner some night?"

Surprised again, Brie shook her head. "The diner is a public place, but I'm not looking for any entanglements."

"Hey, great. Me neither."

She sighed internally. Carey's frequent and fleeting relationships with half the women in Moriah's Landing were well-known. She wasn't particularly flattered to learn she had finally captured his interest.

"Thanks for the ride." As she opened the car door, her skirt tangled on the seat belt latch. Pulling it free she waved and shut the door. Something tumbled to the grass at her feet. A fragile gold necklace with a broken clasp and an expensive-looking pendant glittered up at her.

"Carey, I think one of your lady friends may have lost this."

But the car was already halfway down the hill. Brie stared at the broken necklace. She had a feeling the delicate heart pendant might be made of real rubies and diamonds. It didn't look or feel like costume jewelry. One of his girlfriends was undoubtedly missing the bauble.

Or maybe one of Drew's girlfriends?

Brie refused to dwell on that thought. She'd call Carey and ask him to stop by the diner tomorrow and retrieve the necklace. For now, she'd leave it next to her purse so she wouldn't forget to take it with her tomorrow.

She hoped her mother would hurry home from the vet's. They needed to discuss what they were going to do now that Drew knew about Nicole.

Chapter Eight

Drew returned to the compound and used his cell phone to let his brother know he wouldn't return to help with the float. Leaving his father's car in front of the main house, he walked back to his cottage.

Several times he reached for the telephone to call Brie, but each time, he set the instrument down without dialing. What he needed to say couldn't be said over the phone. He wasn't sure yet exactly what it was he wanted to say. His mind vacillated between shock, outrage and incredible excitement.

He was a father! He couldn't seem to stop thinking about Nicole. One thing was perfectly clear in his mind, he intended to be part of her life from now on. And he couldn't stop wondering if his grandfather had known about Brie's pregnancy. There was only one way to find out.

As Drew opened the door to the main house, he was surprised to discover Carey and Nancy huddled together in the open foyer.

"Drew! There you are. We need to talk to you for a minute."

"I don't have a minute right now, Carey."

"Make one."

Drew paused.

"Maybe we'd better do this in private," Nancy suggested.

Drew looked from one face to another, anxious to go and confront his grandfather. "Just spit it out."

"Fine," Carey said. "Nancy told me that Brianna Dudley has a little girl."

Drew gave Nancy a hard look, angry that she shared that information after he'd asked her not to say anything.

"I know. She's my daughter, Carey."

"What the devil are you talking about?"

Drew swung around. Maureen and William Pierce were descending the open staircase. His mother's shocked expression said they had heard every word. And his brother came inside behind him.

"Let's move this discussion to the office," Drew suggested.

"What discussion?" Zach asked.

"Never mind," his father snapped.

Zach's body tightened. Drew saw the hurt behind his shuttered expression. "On the contrary," Drew told his father. "Zach isn't a kid anymore. This affects all of us, one way or another."

"Do you mean to say it's true?" his mother asked.

"Yes. I'm going to ask Brie to marry me."

His mother gasped. Hastily, she clamped a hand over her lips. Nancy inhaled sharply. Carey, his father and Zach all gaped at him with identical expressions.

Then the hall exploded in raised voices, bringing Anton Pierce from the library. Drew's father wasted no time in telling him the news.

Drew was finally able to move everyone to the office, where he waited for the uproar to die down—only it

never did. His father paced the floor angrily. His mother
sank into a chair in the corner twisting her opal ring
around and around. Zach leaned against the bookcase.
Carey plopped unhappily into a chair next to the cre-
denza and stared at the heavy gilt frame on the opposite
wall. Only Nancy stood apart, frowning.

"You cannot mean to marry a waitress," his grandfather decreed for the third time in as many minutes.

"Andrew, marriage is totally unnecessary. Even
Nancy's investigator says there is no father listed on the
birth certificate. We can pay her—"

"Enough!" Drew stared his father down until the
senator's words sputtered into silence and the pacing
stopped. Next, his gaze went to his grandfather. The
fierce light of battle faded more slowly from those
canny, tired eyes, but the once-powerful man sitting in
the padded leather chair leaned back, looking oddly de-
feated.

Nancy Bell's expression held regret, disappointment
and acceptance. Carey stared vacantly, rubbing his chin
as if it were a talisman. Only Zach offered a wink, a
smile and a thumbs-up of encouragement. Drew felt
closer to his brother in that moment than ever before.
But it was his mother who stunned them all. Always
prim and excessively reserved, she stood regally and
glided forward, laying a hand on his arm.

"Very well. If we're going to have a wedding we'd
best get started with the arrangements. I'll need to get
her properly attired," his mother stated calmly. "There
isn't time to take her into Boston and have it done right,
but I can call in a few favors to get things started. I
think it would be best to have a quiet wedding, don't
you? Perhaps here in the garden if that meets with your

approval. It's quite lovely right now thanks to all the rain this year.''

"Thank you, Mother, but—''

She gazed at him with eyes the same intense shade as his own. The same blue as his daughter's.

"Tell me one thing, Drew. Does she look like Tasha?''

The very room seemed to inhale. Drew felt as if unseen generations were waiting expectantly for his pronouncement.

"No, mother,'' he said gently. "Nicole looks like Brie. Except for her eyes. She has our eyes.''

His mother inclined her head. "Very well. How soon do you plan to hold the wedding, Andrew?''

"Maureen!'' William Pierce protested sharply. "All this talk of weddings is nonsense. Drew isn't thinking straight. The bottom line is that he can't possibly *marry* the girl. She works in a *diner*. She lives down by the wharf!''

"So did I, once,'' Maureen said with quiet dignity.

His prim, cultured mother had once lived in Brie's neighborhood?

"While we would all prefer to forget that fact, it's the simple truth.'' She turned to Anton Pierce. "And I didn't turn out so badly, did I?''

The old man rose slowly, walked to the humidor and removed a cigar. "No,'' he agreed quietly. "You didn't. I objected to your marriage. Strongly, as I recall. But it was because I'd hoped William would forge a stronger political alliance for the sake of his career. Just as I had hoped Andrew might.'' He sighed and regarded Nancy with obvious regret. "We'll need to come up with a plan to put the best spin on this situation that we can,'' he stated, some of his natural arrogance returning. "That will be your job, Nancy."

"Excuse me," Drew interrupted before they could get carried away planning his life again. "We're being a bit premature here. I haven't asked Brie to marry me yet."

"A formality." His grandfather declared. He snipped off the end of his chosen cigar.

"Not if she says no."

"Don't be ridiculous," his father sputtered. "How could she say no?"

Drew stared at his father without really seeing him. "What worries me," he said softly, "is why she'd say yes."

PAMELA DUDLEY went upstairs to read shortly after nine. She'd taken the news about Leland Manning's procedure with little enthusiasm.

"We can't afford it."

"I'll find a way, Mom."

"You've done enough. Some things are meant to be."

"You can't give up. I won't let you. Nicole and I need you. We have to try everything. You know we do. Monday morning I'll talk with the bank. I'll see what we can arrange."

Her mother's sudden tears nearly broke her heart.

Brie had spent hours since then simply staring out the window at the empty darkness. "If only we really were witches with powers." She and her mother could stop worrying about what Drew would do about Nicole. And Brie could cast a spell that would heal her mother once and for all. But wishing wouldn't make it so.

As if sensing her despair, Max jumped onto her lap.

She stroked his soft fur in gratitude. "You wouldn't happen to know any spells, would you, boy?"

There had to be a way to get the money Manning wanted. She would do anything. Anything at all. Closing her eyes, she tried not to wonder for the millionth time what Drew was going to do.

The telephone rang, startling her. She hastened to lift the receiver before it woke her mother. "Hello?"

"Brie? It's Drew. Did I wake you?"

Brie stiffened. Max jumped down with a mew of disgust.

"I didn't mean to call so late."

She gripped the telephone, determined not to let any trace of emotion show in her voice. "I have to be at work at six," she told him. "We'll be busy because of the parade."

"The diner always closes right afterward, doesn't it?"

"Yes," she admitted reluctantly.

"Would you meet me in the park after the parade?"

Brie wondered if she was imagining the note of uncertainty in Drew's tone.

"I could send a car."

"I'd rather walk," she said quickly.

"I know."

She pictured him running a hand through his hair.

"I'm sorry I walked off like that this afternoon. I needed some time to think."

She gripped the phone more tightly. "And now you've come to a decision?"

"I know what I want," he said firmly, "But any decisions need to be mutual from now on. Look, it's late. We'll talk tomorrow. I'll let you go back to sleep now. Good night."

Numb with apprehension, Brie held the phone long after Drew hung up.

What had he decided? They could hardly hold a private conversation in the middle of the park. What was Drew thinking? Brie set down the phone and turned back to the window with an aching heart.

Max startled her by leaping onto the back of her chair and uttering a low growl as he stared out the window. His tail swished angrily.

Brie strained to see through the screen. The street was dark. Several of the old trees had overrun the streetlight and the mayor hadn't responded to calls asking for them to be pruned back.

Nothing moved, but Max was right. She sensed a presence hiding in the shadows.

Max flattened his ears and rumbled a low feline sound of anger. Brie reached for the telephone. She couldn't force her eyes from the window.

"Nine-one-one. What is the nature of your emergency?"

"There may be a prowler outside my mother's house."

MINUTES CREPT PAST BEFORE a car sped down the street, stopping out front. Not a police car, but a vehicle Brie recognized. Cullen Ryan stepped from the sedan and started for her front porch. Abruptly, he stopped.

"Hold it right there. Police," he yelled. Brianna's heart leaped to her throat as Cullen took off running, disappearing between the houses.

The passenger door opened and his wife, Elizabeth, ran up the sidewalk. Incredibly relieved at the sight of her friend, Brie rushed to open the front door.

"Elizabeth!"

"Are you okay, Brie?"

"I'm fine." But as they hugged, she realized she was shaking. "It's so good to see you."

"Same here."

Elizabeth gave a startled exclamation. Max was stropping her legs in greeting.

"Max, you beautiful devil, you scared me. How are you doing, fellow?"

She bent to lift the cat when a form suddenly appeared at the edge of the porch. Both women jumped and Max skittered back inside. Cullen mounted the steps in twos.

"I thought I told you to wait in the car," he chided his new bride.

"I know, but when you took off, I knew Brie would be upset. Did he get away?"

"Afraid so," he said ruefully. "I'd like to have a look around the house, if you don't mind, Brie."

"I'd like that, too. I was just about to lock up for the night."

"You didn't get a good view of him?"

"No. Actually, it was Max who warned me someone was out there."

"Good boy, Max. A real watch-cat, huh?"

"Max is a very smart cat. Come in, both of you."

Brie was grateful for her friend's presence as Cullen walked around, checking doors and locking windows for her.

"I've missed you," Elizabeth said. "We've barely seen each other since the wedding."

"I know. I'm sorry. I've been busy."

"Me, too. Are you doing okay?"

"Sure." Her life was about to explode into a possible public scandal, her mother was dying and she had people taking her picture and shooting at her—not to mention prowlers outside her window. Otherwise, Brie decided, she was doing just fine.

"How's Nicole?"

Fitzwiggy let out a squawk of disgruntled protest as Cullen moved around the kitchen, disturbing him.

"Nicole's fine."

"Oh, good."

"We really need to catch up. Why don't you bring her over one evening? I'll invite my little brother, Brandon, and the kids can play."

"I'd like that," Brie agreed. Elizabeth spent as much of her time as possible with her four-year-old brother. Brandon was a genius like his sister, but Elizabeth was determined to see to it that her brother grew up feeling loved for who he was, and not just how intelligent he was.

"All set, Brie," Cullen said. "Everything's locked down. I checked around outside, as well. Whatever the creep was planning, he didn't have a chance to do anything."

"Thanks, Cullen. Would you like something to drink?"

"No, thanks. We need to get home. Tomorrow's going to be a long day with the parade and all the festivities."

"You're working?"

"Everyone's working tomorrow. Elizabeth and I were on our way home from the store when I heard the call go out. As soon as I recognized your address I offered to come. I only wish I'd caught the guy. I'd really like to get my hands on the ones responsible for all the mischief around here lately."

Brie wanted to tell Cullen she didn't think the watcher had mischief in mind. There had been something brooding and evil outside tonight. But she held her tongue, afraid he'd think she was being imaginative.

"Brie, are you sure you're okay?" Elizabeth asked again.

"Just a little edgy."

Cullen frowned. "Why don't you pack up Nicole and your mom and come and stay at our place tonight?"

"That's nice of you, Cullen, but no. Thank you."

"Are you sure, Brie?" Elizabeth asked. "We wouldn't mind."

"You're good friends, but I'm sure we'll be fine now that Cullen scared him off."

Cullen smiled as he gazed around the room. Abruptly the smiled vanished. A hard look came over his features. He strode to the end table where Brie's purse was sitting.

"Oh!" Elizabeth gasped as he held up the broken necklace Brie had set beside her purse so she'd remember to take it with her in the morning.

Cullen went from friend to cop in an instant. "Where did you get this, Brie?"

"It fell out of Drew's car when Carey dropped me off. Why?"

Cullen cursed.

"Leland Manning claims his wife was wearing a necklace exactly like this one when she was kidnapped."

DREW CLIMBED ABOARD the float, his eyes gritty from lack of sleep. Nerves played havoc with his stomach. He'd had second and third thoughts about this plan of his, but there was no turning back now.

He adjusted his hat as the tractor started up. Dressed as his forefather, Drew took his position as the float lurched forward. And the tractor stuttered to a sudden, jarring halt.

Drew watched the commotion for several minutes before climbing down. "What's wrong?"

"Sorry, Drew," the driver said. "I think someone put sand or sugar in the gas tank. This baby isn't going anywhere."

Faces fell all around him. His crew had worked hard and the float looked fantastic. "Okay, guys, let's get the lines unhooked."

"What are you going to do?" Zach asked. "There isn't time to bring in another tractor. Do you know someone with a truck and a trailer hitch?"

"Nope. We're going to do it the hard way."

THE LOCALS ESTABLISHED their territory early at the diner, staking out the best booths for a comfortable view of the parade. Brie was running on adrenaline this morning after pacing the house most of the night. She hadn't called the police again, but the sense that something still lurked in the darkness out of sight never left her. Added to her other worries, sleep had been impossible.

Maybe the storytellers were right. Maybe McFarland Leary's ghost did rise from his grave every five years, wreaking vengeance on the town. After all, during the height of the witch trials they had hung him in a public assembly right there on the village green for associating with a known "witch." The tale claimed he faced his accusers with his head high, his eyes blazing in fury. In a quiet voice that carried clearly to every man, woman and child, he pronounced his curse, vowing retribution on Moriah's Landing and its heirs. And the sky began to darken. History claims that at the moment of his death, a cloud swallowed the sun and a terrible storm swept inland, sending everyone running for shelter. Thus his legend was insured and for many locals, McFarland Leary's name became synonymous with the bogeyman.

Brie wasn't sure how much of the legend was true, but she'd begun to wonder. The night of their hazing in the cemetery five years ago, it had seemed like she and her friends had unleashed something terrible. Certainly none of their lives had ever been the same afterward. And now, five years later, dramatic changes were happening once more.

"Will you look at that?" someone exclaimed.

"Is that Andrew Pierce?"

"I think so," another voice agreed. "It's the Pierce family float."

Brie glimpsed the float causing all the comment. Dressed in full Pilgrim costume, Drew led a group of similarly attired people who were pushing and pulling the vibrantly decorated flatbed wagon housing their float. The theme depicted the first landing amid a storm-tossed sea. Obviously, Drew represented the founding father.

Not a bad strategy for someone running for mayor. Brie wondered if they were pulling the float as a subtle message to remind people of the struggle the founding fathers had met in their attempt to build the town, or if they wanted to establish how the town had to pull together to accomplish a goal. Either way, they were making a huge—and favorable—impact.

The float was nearly past when something exploded directly in Drew's path. What sounded like a series of firecrackers sent people running in all directions. Smoke obliterated the scene as several smoke bombs were lobbed into the street. Girls from the riding academy had been right behind Drew's float, each one carrying a flag and pole. Horses shied and reared in fright. One girl was unseated. Her horse bolted into the crowd. People screamed as the parade erupted in chaos.

Nicole!

Brie's mother had planned to walk down the hill with her granddaughter at the start of the parade. As people stampeded toward the diner's small front entrance, Brie pivoted and ran to the steps off the deck.

Smoke rose slowly in the heavy, humid air. Kat's younger sister, Emily, sat on the ground holding her arm. Blood ran between her fingers. Brie saw Drew's brother, Zachary, rush to her side. He lifted her tenderly, peering around wildly.

"Zach! Use the deck out back," Brie called to him. "Have Lois call the paramedics."

Brie pushed her way through the crowd. She saw Drew trying to calm the riderless horse who was dangerously close to a group of frightened young children. Spotting her neighbors, she ran over to the couple.

"Have you seen Nicole or my mother?"

"They were down at the end of our street."

Brie relaxed. That was far enough from the disturbance. The police were restoring order quickly. Searching for her mother in this mob was useless, so she headed back to the diner.

Others had followed Zach, seeking refuge on the back deck. Lois and Sam, the cook, were administering first aid with the help of the newly hired busboy. Zach sat at a table with Emily, pressing a towel against her arm. He looked up as Brie started across the deck.

"I think Emily was shot."

DREW CROUCHED DOWN instinctively when the first smoke bomb detonated. Almost at the same time, his hat sailed away. Smoke clouded his view as people began screaming. A riderless horse nearly knocked him over in its panicked frenzy. Drew bolted after it, reaching for the dangling reins.

He thought he glimpsed Brie in the crowd once, but she disappeared before he could call out to her. Finally, the police restored order and Drew gazed around. His hat lay in the gutter. A neat round hole ran from one side to the other. Brie had been right. Someone wanted him dead.

Chapter Nine

Brie rushed home as soon as the diner closed. She was almost at the house when her mother's voice called to her from two doors down. Pamela and Nicole were sitting on Mary Jackson's front porch drinking lemonade. Nicole was playing with her friends and the little girls were giggling as they watched Little Imp tussle with a ball of yarn. Relief made Brie's knees weak.

"I wasn't expecting you home," her mother said calmly. "Weren't you supposed to go somewhere after work?"

Drew! She'd forgotten all about meeting him after the parade.

"I, uh, decided to change first. Did you go to the parade?"

"Only for a few minutes. It was too hot. Besides, Nicole was upset over leaving Little Imp behind, so when I bumped into Mary and her girls, we decided to come back here instead."

"We plan to take the girls over later to watch the fireworks," Mary added. "Sure sounded like a lot of commotion a while ago."

Brianna quietly told them what had happened in front of the diner.

"I don't understand what's wrong with people anymore. I was just telling Mary about the prowler we had last night."

"What sort of prowler thinks he's going to find anything worth stealing in this neighborhood, I ask you? Maybe McFarland Leary rose from his grave, after all," Mary suggested. "You have to admit, there have been some strange and horrible things happening in town these past few months."

"I don't think a ghost threw smoke bombs into the crowd. Mom, please keep a close eye on Nicole. I'm feeling real edgy and I have to see someone."

Her mother nodded knowingly.

"I should be back shortly."

"Your mother will stay right here with me," Mary announced firmly. "My Henry will be home soon."

Although she was already late, Brie took time to shower and change, pulling on a crisp blue-and-white sundress. Though faded, the comfortable shirtwaist made her feel more feminine. There wasn't time to worry about her hair so she toweled it dry, fluffed it with a comb, and found her mother's wide-brimmed floppy white hat to cover most of it. Adding sunscreen and a touch of lipstick, she slipped on her sandals and set off for the park.

The dense overgrowth of trees offered shade, but the park bustled with so much activity that the heat and humidity were miserable. Large grills were in operation all over, filling the sluggish air with food odors.

Mayor Thane was at the microphone denouncing the people responsible for this morning's attack. His words had an oddly rehearsed sound to Brie, who barely listened as she scanned the crowd for a glimpse of Drew.

William and Maureen Pierce sat together in the gazebo, next to Chief Redfern and Anton Pierce. There was no sign of Drew.

"I was afraid you weren't coming."

Her heart rate tripled as Drew found her. "Aren't you supposed to be up there with the other speakers?"

"Come with me."

The gentle tug on her arm was nothing compared with the tug on her foolish heart. Brie planted her feet. "I can't go up there!"

"I know. Just stand near the front. Please? We'll talk when I'm finished. My speech is mercifully short."

Though she wanted to refuse, Brie let herself be led to the side of the makeshift stage in front of the gazebo. A scattering of applause indicated the mayor had introduced William Pierce.

Becca Smith stood in the crowd next to Zach. Brie stepped over to join them as Drew hurried onto the stage. "How's Emily, Zach?"

His features lit at Emily's name, but sobered instantly. "She's fine. Her arm bled a lot, but she was just grazed. Chief Redfern insists she got cut by something flying out of the crowd."

Brie lowered her voice. "You don't agree."

"Nope. Neither does her sister, Kat. She took Em to the hospital to get checked out. I'm going over there as soon as Drew finishes his talk. Shh. He's up now."

There was an underlying edge of excitement that surprised Brie. Zach gave her a broad grin and turned his attention back to the dais.

Andrew Pierce had been born for politics. With his easy confidence, that heart-stopping smile and his open charisma, he had the crowd's full attention in seconds. "I'm going to beg your indulgence while I depart from the usual patter."

He looked directly at Brie. Her stomach gave a strange little flip. He smiled and his gaze roved back over the crowd.

"As all of you know, I come from a long line of politicians and lawyers. Our success depends on our ability to talk. Everyone knows both professions are filled with a lot of hot air."

People tittered. A couple of male voices called out something Brie couldn't hear. Drew grinned infectiously. Then his expression turned serious. "Four years ago, there was a question I should have asked someone. To my regret, I didn't."

He held everyone captive with the intensity behind his words.

"Five simple but terribly important words, and I've racked my brain for a way to ask this question. Our family has been part of this town since its inception. You are our friends, our neighbors, our classmates, the people we care about. I decided to ask my question publicly, with all of you standing in witness."

Her mouth went dry. Drew looked directly at her once more.

"Brianna Dudley, will you marry me?"

"That was six words," Zach murmured, grinning. "But who cares? Way to go, big brother."

Deafened by the blood pounding through her head, she was prodded forward until she stood directly in front of Drew at the foot of the makeshift stand.

"Please don't say no," he begged softly.

She wanted to weep. She wanted to fly at him in a rage. She wanted to run. Instead, her dazed brain let him slide a large ring onto her finger and fold her into his arms while the crowd went wild.

Panic filled her as people crowded around offering

congratulations and best wishes. If Drew had released his tight hold even for a second she would have fled. She saw Becca smiling encouragingly at her. Somehow that gesture of friendship steadied her. And just in time, as Frederick Thane suddenly cut off her view.

"Nice little bit of upstaging there, Pierce." His voice was hearty, but his eyes glittered with the promise of retribution. "Congratulations."

He hated Drew, she realized.

Enough to kill him?

"Best of luck to you, too, my dear," he said with false cheer. Her skin prickled as he pumped her hand. She thought she heard him whisper "You're going to need it," as he moved away.

Her heart stuttered to a stop as Anton Pierce took his place. She hadn't seen the older man up close since that day in his home when she'd accepted his money to pay her mother's medical bills. The years had not been kind. Anton Pierce looked every one of his eighty-odd years, though his eyes still gleamed with the power and intensity she remembered.

Unconsciously, Brie lifted her chin in silent defiance. She would not cower. She'd kept her word. If he thought this was her idea...

His lips curved just the tiniest bit. She would have sworn that was approval glinting in his eyes.

"As you get older you'll realize life holds some funny cards up its sleeve," he told her. "I've found it's best to be prepared to make allowances. Welcome to the family, Brianna."

"Close your mouth, Brie," Zach whispered at her back. "He doesn't bite in public."

For the life of her, she couldn't think of a single thing

to say. He moved away with a sad smile and William and Maureen Pierce took his place.

"Brianna." There was no warmth in William Pierce's brief handshake. She'd only met him once or twice and she hadn't much cared for the stuffy politician.

Maureen edged him aside. Perfectly attired as always, she had quite startling blue eyes. Brie hadn't realized Drew's mother shared the same intense eye color as Nicole and Drew.

"Is your daughter with you? I'm anxious to meet her."

Brie looked frantically to Drew. His mother knew about Nicole? He squeezed her waist in reassurance.

"No, I…she's at home…with my mother."

"Of course. It is warm out here for the little ones, isn't it?" She smiled brightly and stepped forward to hug Brie. Standing frozen with shock in the unexpected embrace, Brie realized people were taking pictures. Reporters were firing questions. She pulled herself together long enough to return the hug, noting Maureen's approval, even as she prayed the ordeal would end.

No one was answering prayers today.

Drew tried to extract them from the crowd without success. He should have known Brie was too private a person for such a public display. Why had he thought this was such a good idea last night? Sure, it deflected the blackmailer and ruined whatever plan Frederick Thane had in mind, but at what cost? Someone had shot at him this morning. Had he just made Brie a target as well?

It was Cullen Ryan who came to his aid.

"Congratulations." He eyed Brie closely. "I just spoke to Elizabeth. She told me to tell you if you didn't call her tonight she'd throttle you. Her words. Look, I hate to interrupt right now, but I really need to talk with you both.''

"If you can get us out of here, we're in your debt,'' Drew told him. Brie gazed up in surprise. It was the first time she'd actually looked at him since he'd slipped his grandmother's ring on her finger.

"Come on. We'll go to the station.''

THE POLICE STATION was empty save the dispatcher. Cullen waved and led them back to his cubicle.

"You were right, Drew. Someone fired four rounds into the crowd this morning. Young Emily Ridgemont was grazed, and that's a scary hole through your hat, but—''

Brie gasped. Drew squeezed her hand reassuringly.

"—it doesn't appear anyone was seriously injured. We found four spent cartridges. He used a rifle.''

"But Zach said Chief Redfern—''

"Hasn't seen my report yet.'' From a desk drawer he retrieved a clear plastic envelope. "What can you tell me about this, Drew?''

Brie perched on the edge of her seat, staring at the necklace inside the envelope as though it was going to turn into a snake and bite her.

Drew lifted the packet. "I'm no jeweler, but I'd say this is eighteen-karat gold, good-quality rubies and diamonds. It probably cost somewhere in the neighborhood of—''

"Have you ever seen it before?''

"No.''

Their gazes locked. Finally, Cullen sat back with a nod.

"You claimed you never met Ursula Manning.''

"That's right. My uncle's done some work with Leland Manning."

Cullen nodded. "I'm going to tell you a couple of things in confidence. They aren't to be repeated to anyone. There are enough wild rumors going around town right now." He ran a tired hand through his hair. "I got the ballistics report back."

Drew leaned forward.

"Ursula Manning was killed by a rifle."

"We were all firing handguns."

"Someone wasn't. The shooter was in the woods above the firing range."

Drew cursed. "I saw Leland Manning at the fence right after the shooting."

"So you said. Manning claims that it's near the place where he was told to put the ransom money."

"David Bryson was in the woods. too."

"We're checking on him." The detective hesitated. "Manning believes his wife was having an affair with someone."

Drew looked from the necklace to the detective. "You thought I was that someone?"

"Several reliable witnesses saw her in your green sports car on more than one occasion."

Drew sighed. "Carey."

"Carey Eldrich?"

"He's been driving the car for several weeks. He has...something of a reputation—"

"I know all about his reputation."

With a heavy heart, Drew told how Carey had disappeared for a long time that morning, claiming to be ill. "But if she was shot with a rifle, he couldn't have shot her."

"No. He couldn't."

"Razz could have."

Both men stared at Brie.

"Razz and Dodie were talking in the diner after the shooting."

Ryan made notes as she told him what she knew about the pair. Then Drew told him about the incident outside the Dudley house and Leland Manning's threat against him.

"You never told me about that," Brie accused.

"Just like you didn't tell me about your prowler last night."

"And neither of you told me about getting shot at the other night," Cullen said.

With a guilty shrug, Drew filled him in and they both answered questions while Cullen took notes.

"So, now what?" Brie asked.

"I'm going to move you and your mother and Nicole out to the compound today, for one thing," Drew said.

"You most certainly will not."

"You'd be safe there. Nancy is staying at the main house so the other guest cottage is empty."

"You think stone walls and fences are going to make us safe? I don't think so. Whoever was in my yard last night didn't do anything, but he could have. I was standing right in front of the window. I'd be dead if that had been his intention."

"I don't care. I won't have you and my daughter at risk."

"Will you listen to the man," she said to Cullen. "He's the one getting shot at!"

"And like a damn fool I just made you a target in front of the whole town! If someone wants to get to me, they now know they can do it through you. We're getting married tomorrow as soon as the town hall opens."

"We are not!" She pulled the loose ring from her finger and held it out. "I never agreed to marry you at all!"

"You have to marry me!"

"Why?"

"Because…you have my daughter."

Drew instantly regretted his words. Something infinitely sad came and went in her eyes.

"Brie, I'm sorry. I went about this all wrong."

"Yes. You did."

Ryan's chair creaked as he leaned back. Drew had forgotten about him. So, apparently, had Brie. Red seeped up her neck. With shaking fingers, she put the ring back on her finger.

"Sorry, Cullen," she said. "We can have this fight later."

"No apology is necessary."

"Yeah, it is," Drew said. Brie sat stiffly beside him looking grim and hurt. This wasn't how he'd wanted things to go.

"Maybe you were right," he told her quietly. "Maybe it is a character flaw, but I'm going to apologize to you, anyhow. I'm sorry, Brie. I screwed up. Again. Please marry me. Let me take care of you and your mother. I want to get to know our daughter. You can finish your schooling, go on to law school. I can help you if you'll let me. You won't ever have to worry about money again."

"Ha! My mother needs some very expensive experimental treatments." Her voice cracked. "She's dying, Drew."

He covered her hand. "I know. I'll open you a checking account first thing tomorrow morning. We'll go to Boston, see a specialist—"

"She has a good doctor."

"Whatever you need, Brie. Whatever she needs."

She stared at the ring on her finger.

"It belonged to my father's mother," he told her. "I didn't have time to buy you a new one. We can pick out something more to your taste tomorrow."

"The ring is beautiful." She stared at it wistfully.

"Then we'll get it sized so it fits."

"I'm not getting married at city hall tomorrow."

"Okay. My mother offered her garden. She says lots of flowers are in bloom right now."

Brie looked up at him, her face expressionless. "All right."

Relieved, he pulled her into a hug. Her body gradually relaxed and she hugged him back. But a question niggled at the back of his mind.

Why had she said yes?

Chapter Ten

"Becca, I need help."

"Brie! Hi! What are you doing here? Aren't you supposed to be at work?"

"Sure, if I still had a job, which thanks to Drew I don't anymore."

Becca tipped her head. "Trouble in paradise?"

"I know nothing about paradise, but I can tell you plenty about the opposite end of the spectrum. Drew actually called my boss to say I wouldn't be working there any longer."

"Ouch. I imagine you had a few things to say in response."

"Most of it unrepeatable, not that it changed anything."

"You sound like you need a friend. How about a cup of tea?"

"It's ninety-eight degrees outside."

"So we'll put some ice in it."

The two women shared a laugh. Becca led her to the back office. A tiny table with two chairs and an electric teapot sat there. She gestured for Brie to have a seat. "Tell me about your plans for the wedding."

"I don't have any plans. You'll have to ask Drew's mother."

"Uh-oh."

"Yeah. Becca, I've been buying my own clothing since I was twelve. Suddenly I don't know how to dress, or wear my hair or put on makeup or—" She took a deep breath, surprised to find herself so near tears. "I know Maureen is only trying to help, but if Drew wanted a Barbie doll to dress he should have bought one of them instead of me."

Brie stopped as she realized what she'd said. Becca went to a small cupboard and pulled out a pastry box and some tea bags.

"Sit back and relax for a few minutes."

"I can't, I have to get my mother to Leland Manning's place for her first treatment at one o'clock, and—"

"Then we have plenty of time. I don't have any appointments coming in this morning." She opened the box and poured hot water over the tea bags. "Now tell me how I can help."

"I'm in over my head, Becca. Maureen insists I need a total makeover. She took me to a nail salon yesterday!"

"Nice job."

"Nice? I've never in my life had nails like these. They hurt. Don't laugh, I think the woman put them on with cement. Look, I know Maureen means well, and she's always dressed impeccably, but—"

"Her taste and style aren't yours."

"Exactly. Do you know what her idea of a small garden wedding is? Five hundred people! I don't even *know* five hundred people! And I'm exhausted from talking to these Boston designers she keeps calling.

They've been sending me books and sketches and samples until my head's ready to burst. Can you see me in miles of taffeta with puffy sleeves? Just look in this bag at these samples—''

''Here, try one of these pastries, they're sinful. Let's see what you have here. Plaid?''

''Oh, this isn't just for the wedding. According to Maureen, I have to have an entire wardrobe for political functions. Seven suits, she says. I hate suits. They make me look blocky.''

''Take another sip of tea. I'd have to agree, suits aren't your style, they're hers. You need simple styles and colors that will flatter your hair and skin tones. No blacks, nothing in white.''

''Except the wedding dress,'' she said morosely.

''Not even. Soft ivory, in my opinion. Something simple with a long, elegant drape. Maybe a variation on a Grecian drape or something that would leave your shoulders bare. In this heat, you're going to want something cool and simple. What about something like this?''

Quickly she sketched a design on the back of a napkin. Brie inhaled sharply.

''Oh, my gosh, I dreamed of a wedding gown almost exactly like that when I was young. Elizabeth and Tasha and I were going through a catalog one day, you know, just sort of talking about what kind of wedding dress we'd like to wear. And that's it! Almost exactly as I pictured! Mom was right. She suggested I come and see you and Maureen agreed. Do you think we can find something like this in time?''

''I can make it for you.''

''But the wedding's in two weeks!''

''That's enough time. Now, let's see...''

Being with Becca was like being back in college. The two of them were giggling helplessly over a pattern when they heard someone enter the shop.

Becca looked up from the bolt of fabric she'd just carried to the table. "Uh-oh. It's Drew."

Panic hit her. Brie began stuffing the samples and design patterns back into the tote bag. "What time is it?"

"Twelve-thirty-seven," Drew said, sounding amused.

"It can't be! I have to pick up my mother!"

Her mother had shocked her by agreeing to move to the Pierce compound temporarily. Brie felt as if she were riding a tidal wave from the moment Drew began speaking to the crowd on the Fourth of July. Any minute now she'd fall in and drown.

Drew filled the office doorway, looking formidable and more sinful than the pastries they'd been eating. "Fortunately, your mother's appointment was postponed until tomorrow morning." He eyed the remaining confections and lifted a chocolate pastry. Brie watched as his strong white teeth sank into the gooey treat. Her heart pounded out of control for no reason whatsoever. There was nothing at all sexy about chewing and swallowing.

"This stuff should be illegal," he said, looking into her eyes. "Melts in the mouth."

That wasn't the only thing melting. Why did this keep happening to her? All she had to do was look at him and she wanted him. She would be the happiest bride on the planet if he was marrying her out of love instead of trying to save his political career. But then, wasn't she marrying him to save her mother and keep her daughter?

"My mother's been giving you a hard time, hasn't she?" Drew asked.

"Of course not. She's trying to help me be presentable."

"You're presentable just the way you are, Brie."

A thrill of a pleasure curled in her belly.

"Mom appreciates your help, Rebecca. She's been quite impressed with your work and she's feeling guilty for overwhelming Brie."

"She hasn't overwhelmed me," Brie lied quickly, not wanting to cause a rift between mother and son. "Look, this is the dress Becca's offered to make for the wedding. Isn't it fabulous?"

"Fabulous," he agreed. But he looked at her instead of the picture Becca had drawn. Maybe she was crazy, but Brie could swear he was flirting with her. Of course that was ridiculous. And yet...

They hadn't had five minutes alone since the announcement, though they'd been together every day. Drew had spent most of his spare time getting to know his daughter. The results were obvious and immediate. Nicole had instantly succumbed to the famous Andrew Pierce charisma. Her face lit up whenever Drew appeared. Even Brie's mother had a similar reaction to his presence. It seemed all the Dudley women were doomed to fall for Drew.

"Since you have your afternoon free now, and I've managed to clear my calendar for the rest of the day, I thought we could spend it together."

"Why?"

Disappointment flared in his eyes. "That's what engaged couples generally do."

"But we're not..."

"Not what?"

He was standing too close. The only thing she could think of was how badly she'd like to slide her hands across his chest and pull him a whole lot closer. How crazy was that?

"Like other couples?" he finished.

"Yes." It came out a breathless whisper.

"Would you like to be?"

Oh, yes. To have him love her the way she—

"Come on, let's take a ride. I want to show you something. Becca, will you excuse us?"

Becca smiled as she pretended to fan herself. "Absolutely."

Drew grinned. "If Becca doesn't mind, she can call my mother and tell her what works. And Becca, make sure to send my mother a substantial bill for your time."

"Oh, no, Brie is—"

"My mother can afford it and this was entirely her idea. Let her foot the bill. And Brie, I've warned her that if her pet hairdresser even hints that you'd look good with short hair, I'll restyle his face."

Becca gave a mock sigh. "I just love a forceful man."

"Brat," he teased. "Come on, Brie."

She let him lead her outside, not sure what to make of this playful Drew. "I happen to look good with short hair," she said.

Drew chuckled. "I'm sure you do, but I love your hair long and wild, tumbling around your shoulders. I'd like it even better spread on my chest."

Brie thought this was a really stupid time to feel faint, but the picture of him naked beneath her, their bodies pressed together, was a little more than she felt prepared to handle. "You're confusing me."

"Am I?"

He kept looking at her the way she'd looked at those pastries. Her stomach was turning somersaults.

"Nicole—"

"Is occupied for the afternoon," he said smugly. "Elizabeth brought her brother Brandon over to play this afternoon."

"But I should—"

He swung her around so their bodies touched, lifted her chin with a knuckle, slanting his mouth over hers. Hormones kicked to life with reckless abandon as the world spun away. He deepened the kiss, drawing her body snugly against his own in a fit so natural, so perfect, she couldn't think of anything but how much she wanted him.

"You should come with me," he said against her mouth.

"Honey, if I were a few years younger, I'd go with the man. Good-looking piece of beefcake like that. I'd teach him a thing or two."

They broke apart. Arabella Leigh watched them through rheumy eyes. She had to be in her late eighties if she was a day. A bit senile, Arabella generally walked the wharf, but it wasn't unusual to see her just about anywhere around town, mumbling to herself or talking to anyone she met.

She patted her disheveled gray hair and struck a pose. "What about it, handsome? I'll go with you if she won't."

"If I were a few years older, I might take you up on that offer, Arabella," Drew responded kindly.

Arabella cackled gleefully. With a cheerful wave, she ambled toward the waterfront talking to herself happily. Drew led Brie to a shiny blue car she hadn't seen before.

"How many cars do you own?" she demanded, to cover the flustered feeling inside her.

"This one isn't mine. It's yours. I bought it for you this morning."

Brie froze. "I don't want a car! Take it back! My mother has a perfectly fine car when I need one."

Unperturbed, he shook his head. "That perfectly fine car needs four new tires, a new transmission, shocks, springs and a muffler, not to mention air bags and a safer car seat. This car has all of the above."

"How do you know that?"

"I read the invoice."

"I mean about my mother's car."

"Our mechanic checked it over yesterday."

"I didn't know that."

"You were getting a manicure."

Brie glanced down at her new fake fingernails and resisted an impulse to curl them away out of sight. "I don't see a car seat," Brie told him meekly.

"It's in the trunk."

God, she loved his smile.

"Are you going to fight me on every issue?"

"Probably. Drew, I can't help it. I don't want you giving me things like cars and new clothes."

"Why not?"

"Because it makes me feel inadequate."

Drew realized she was close to tears. The knowledge slid through him like a knife. He was asking so much of her. He hadn't understood until he heard her giggling so freely with Becca Smith.

"You are not inadequate. But you're right, Brie. I'm sorry. I didn't think. I'll take the car back if you want me to. I'll get your mother's car fixed instead. I—"

"No. Please." She laid a hand on his arm. "I'm being stupid and ungrateful. I'm the one who's sorry. This is all wrong. You know it's all wrong. I'm all wrong. You need a wife who dresses right and knows how to do things and—"

Drew swore. "I need you to be yourself, Brie, not a clone of my mother."

She took a half step back at his strident tone. Drew rubbed his jaw, wondering why he kept making such a hash of things. "Will you take a ride with me?"

"All right."

She didn't say another word until he made the turn toward the compound.

"Are we going to your place?"

"In a manner of speaking. The compound is actually comprised of one hundred twenty-seven acres. My family isn't just good at politics, they know how to invest their money and make it grow. They also believe in conservation and planning ahead. Besides this chunk of land, we own beachfront property and several developmental properties in and around Boston and Salem. My great-grandfather was big on acquiring land and buildings. He had a knack for it."

"I didn't realize your holdings were so extensive. You really are rich, aren't you?"

"Does that scare you?"

"It makes me nervous," she admitted.

"Don't be. We've hired on extra security. And look at the good news. No one's shot at me in days."

"That isn't funny! Have you talked to Cullen recently? Has he learned anything?"

"Yesterday, in fact. They're still asking questions. Carey admitted to Cullen that he was having an affair with Ursula Manning," Drew said unhappily. "But he claims he hadn't seen or talked to her in several days prior to the shooting.''

Even though they had both figured as much, Drew was clearly upset. ''Don't you believe him?''

''I want to believe him.''

''You've been friends a long time.''

''I know, but I keep remembering how odd he looked when he finally joined us that morning. He claimed he was sick.''

''Maybe he was.''

''I just found out Carey's family cut him off several weeks ago. He doesn't have a job and he's nearly broke, yet he's been making deposits of cash into his accounts since the murder that he can't, or won't explain.''

''Have you tried talking to him?''

''He won't discuss it.''

''I'm sorry, Drew.'' They sat quietly for a few minutes, lost in thought. Finally, Brie asked, ''Is he still going to be your usher?''

''He hasn't told me any differently.'' Drew stopped where the road ended. He turned off the engine. ''We have to walk from here.''

''Where are we?''

''This is my part of the compound. We're standing on twenty-five acres that were deeded over to me the day after I was born. Each of us were given shares. This section has a natural spring and a brook. I want to show you where I dreamed of building a house one day.''

He took her hand. Her fingers were cold despite the heat. It was a fairly long hike along the hidden deer path, but she didn't complain. It was cooler under the dense canopy of trees. The sound of birds filled the air. He stopped when they reached the clearing, wanting to watch her face when she saw it for the first time. "What do you think?"

Her pleasure was obvious. "It's fantastic. Drew, look," she whispered. A pair of foxes emerged on the other side of the clearing. They tested the wind but didn't scent the human presence. After a moment, three tiny kits came bouncing out of the underbrush and followed their parents to the water's edge.

Drew slid an arm around Brie's waist as they watched the magical scene. The parents stood guard while the kits drank and played. Suddenly coming alert, they urged their family back into the woods.

Brie gazed at him in wonder. "This is a special place."

"I've always thought so."

"I expect to see fairies popping out any second."

He smiled. "Fairies?"

"It feels magical. Don't you sense it? It's charmed."

"Because you're here." He laid a hand over her lips to stop her from saying anything further. "Shh. Don't question the magic."

Leading her to a stone of granite worn smooth on top by whatever force had placed it there, he took his handkerchief and made a production out of dusting it off.

"My lady?"

"But—"

"Shh. No objections. No negativity. Just sit here beside me and let's see what else comes down to the water to drink."

She perched tentatively beside him. After a few minutes she began to relax. He startled her by taking her hand. When she relaxed again he began to rub his thumb against the pad of her hand. A quiver ran down her body.

"What are you doing?"

"Touching you. I like touching you. I always did, remember?"

She tensed. "Drew—"

"Shh. Something's moving over there, see by that tall pine?"

"I don't— Oh! It's a groundhog."

"Fat little sucker, isn't he?"

"That's not very—"

She jumped as he placed a kiss along the back of her neck.

"What are you doing?"

"Kissing you." He trailed a path of light kisses along the collar of her blouse. "This is a magical place. In this circle all things are possible."

She gazed at him with such hope and fear it broke his heart. Sliding his hand gently through her hair, he cupped the back of her head. Very slowly, he brought her face to his. "All things are possible," he whispered against her mouth.

The kiss was gentle. Her body softened. She leaned into him. Need twisted his gut. Slowly the kiss built until it went hot and wild despite his best intentions.

He didn't remember unbuttoning her blouse or unfastening the front clasp that held her bra closed. But when her firm, tempting flesh spilled into his hands, he covered the pink-tipped bud with his mouth and feasted.

She clung to him, making tiny sounds that sent the heat rising even higher in his body. Lured by the scent and taste of her, he sought her mouth, kissing her hard, his tongue penetrating her mouth the way he wanted to penetrate her body. And she kissed him back, her tiny sounds of pleasure twisting his gut into knots of desire so strong he thought he'd die from the need.

He slid his hand inside the waistband of her pants, feeling her belly contract at his touch. Wicked, hot pleasure assailed him, but from somewhere, a core of sanity surfaced.

"We can't," Drew said miserably.

"What?"

Slumberous with molten desire, her green eyes were half closed by passion. Brie shook her head as if trying to understand. Drew withdrew his hand, pulling her body against the wall of his chest.

"I don't have any protection. We already have one child. We aren't going to create another one until we both decide the time is right."

She pulled away and stood, turning her back to him. He watched her fumble with her clothing.

"Brianna." He touched her back lightly. Her spine stiffened beneath his fingers. She walked deeper into the clearing. "I want you so badly I'm shaking, too. I can see you in my mind, hot and naked, and it's making me crazy." His voice broke because he was very much afraid he'd give in to the explosive desire filling his mind and his body.

"We've already made love on a sand dune. Wouldn't you like to try a bed? Our bed—here—in our house? I didn't bring you here to make love to you. I brought you here to share my dream. This is my spot. I'd like to make it our spot. I'm going to put the master bedroom there, where you're standing and— Are you crying?"

"No." She brushed a hand across her face, but she didn't turn around. "We'll put the bedroom where the rock is," she said decisively, though her voice was thick with unshed tears. "I want the kitchen table right here, so we can sit and watch the foxes come and go."

Drew relaxed. Hope rose in his chest. "All right, we'll compromise. When we sit down with the architect, we'll see what he says."

"There's a storm coming."

Drew looked up, seeing nothing but blue sky and a few white clouds. "What?"

She turned to face him. The only trace of passion was the slight puffiness around her lips.

"The pressure's falling. It's coming in fast. We have to get back to the guest house."

Once again he looked to the sky but saw nothing threatening.

"Drew, we have to get back!"

THICK, DARK CLOUDS CHASED across the sky. From his hiding place the man glanced up through the canopy of leaves in surprise as lightning cleaved a jagged path, heralding the rumble of distant thunder. The suddenness of the squall took him by surprise.

He'd been observing the woman and the two children at play, trying to decide if they were alone. The clap of thunder startled the tiny kitten. It scampered directly toward his hiding place. The little boy set off in pursuit. The woman yelled and went after him.

He tensed, preparing to grab his victim. A twig snapped beneath an incautiously placed foot behind him. It could have been an animal, but he knew it wasn't. Someone else was in the woods.

Swearing silently, he slipped away, angrily abandoning his plan. There'd be another time. He'd see to it. His body tightened in anticipation.

THUNDER CRASHED OVERHEAD as Drew drove along the twisty, tree-covered lane to the guest house. Brie suddenly peered out the side window. "Was that Carey?"

"Where?"

"I saw someone in the woods over there. It was just a glimpse, but it looked like him."

"More than likely it was my Uncle Geoffrey. He lives in the guest house on the other side of those trees. He's been skulking about the grounds at odd hours a lot lately."

"How comforting. Why?"

"I've no idea, but I mean to find out. Uncle Geoff's weird, but he's harmless."

At least Drew hoped he was. Drew had been checking into his uncle's activities lately without a lot of success. Some of the rumors were starting to make him distinctly uneasy.

"You know," Brie was saying, "the word *cottage* has a whole different meaning in my part of town. This place is bigger than my mother's house. How many are there?"

"Only three. They were designed to be near the main house, yet give the occupants a full measure of privacy. I'm living in the one in the opposite direction."

"You don't live at the main house?"

"Not since I came home from college. Do you want to see?"

The tension simmering between them since he'd touched her in the clearing rose to the surface once more. Drew watched her breathing quicken, her eyes soften. She was so expressive. He didn't remember much about that night on the beach, but he knew she was a responsive lover.

"Maybe later. I should check on my mom and the kids. She had one of her headaches this morning."

A torrent of rain engulfed the car. Lightning exploded across the sky. As Drew pulled up he saw Pamela Dudley herding two sopping-wet children through the backyard, the bedraggled kitten tucked under her arm.

"Looks like your mom and the kids got caught in the rain." Drew reached for Brie's arm before she could open the door. "About what happened back there in the woods—"

Green fire danced in her eyes. "As I recall, nothing happened other than a couple of kisses. Were you planning to apologize?"

Again.

"Only for not being prepared, but given how you feel about my apologies, I'll settle for promising you that the next time I get you alone in a magical clearing, not even a thunderstorm is going to stop me from making love to you."

Her lips parted in surprise. Her pulse jumped in her throat. His body tightened.

"I'll keep that in mind. Are you coming in?"

"Not right now. But I'll be back."

She nodded jerkily, opened the door and sprinted toward the front of the cottage. Watching her go, Drew wondered how it was he kept blundering so badly around Brie. He was normally accomplished at the art of seduction. It wasn't like him to forget something so elemental as protection. It was almost as if some other force were at work here, determined to keep them apart.

Drew pulled his thoughts from Brie to his uncle. They needed to talk. But no car sat in front of his uncle's cottage. Drew waited for the rain to slow, then ran to the front door. There was no answer and no sound from inside. Twisting the handle, he was disturbed when it gave beneath his fingers.

"Uncle Geoff?" Nothing happened when he flicked on the light switch. The power often went out during thunderstorms. A strange, unpleasant smell permeated the house. Apparently, his uncle had stopped the maids. Even without light, the place needed to be dusted and vacuumed. Dirty dishes were piled everywhere. The stove was splattered with grease and bits of dried food. The smell of rotting garbage made his stomach roil in protest.

The wrongness about the cottage set his teeth on edge. Rain beat a tattoo against the roof and windows as he investigated the bedrooms. His uncle had been using the smallest room as an office, but it had been stripped of everything. In the master bedroom the unmade bed had been slept in, but there wasn't a single personal item anywhere in the room—or, as it turned out—anywhere in the house. His uncle was gone.

Chapter Eleven

Brie had to force herself to sit calmly as Dr. Manning tied the rubber tourniquet around her upper arm. Even here in this brightly lit laboratory on the campus grounds, Leland Manning gave off an aura that was deeply unsettling. The intensity of his stare unnerved her. All she could think about were mad scientists and evil experiments.

As she felt the soft bite of the needle, Brie had the strongest desire to pull her arm back and refuse to allow him to take the promised blood. It didn't matter that he was also going to run the blood test she needed for the wedding. She didn't like Leland Manning. She had to force herself to remain still as her blood ran down the hollow tube of plastic and into the small glass test tube.

"I understand you have a child. A little girl, isn't it?" he asked.

She gazed around at the laboratory, anywhere except those disturbing eyes.

"Yes."

"I was wondering if you'd mind if I took a sample of her blood, as well."

Brie jerked her arm. The needle tore loose and blood welled at the site of the tiny puncture wound.

"I'm sorry, Dr. Manning."

"Quite all right," he said stiffly. "I have enough for my purposes. About your daughter..."

She fought a sense of revulsion. "No! I'm sorry, but Nicole is terrified of needles. She's a worse subject than I am. She can never hold still and I couldn't possibly subject her to having her blood drawn unless it was vital to her health."

"Not even if it meant I could lower the cost of your mother's treatments a bit more?"

"No. I'm sorry."

"Ah, yes, money isn't an issue for you any longer, is it?"

Something in his tone made her stomach constrict. "You know, Dr. Manning, Drew wasn't responsible for your wife's death."

He stared at her coldly. "So the police told me."

His flat tone and stony expression warned her off. "If we're finished, I'll go and check on my mother."

"I've offended you."

No, you've frightened me, but she managed not to say that out loud. Brie shook her head as he applied gauze over the small wound.

"No? Good. I should have the results of your mother's tests back in a few days. Naturally, I'll need to discuss her case with her oncologist before we proceed."

"Dr. Thornton said he'd be more than happy to assist in any way he can."

"Excellent. If all goes well, we can set up a schedule for her early next week."

"Would it affect anything if we wait until after the wedding? Mrs. Pierce has been keeping her rather busy."

"The wedding is next weekend, is it not?"

"Yes. Will you be able to attend?"

"I wouldn't miss it."

She tried not to shudder.

"We shall just hope that tropical depression down south stays put and doesn't turn into a full-scale hurricane. It was on the news this morning. The weather service is monitoring the situation."

No wonder she'd been feeling edgy. Brie reached for her purse. "Dr. Manning, tell me honestly, does my mother have a chance of recovering?"

"Gene therapy is experimental."

"I know. I just wondered—"

"I anticipate the drug will go to the altered cancer cells and force them to become a suicide potion for the cancer itself. Gene therapy is still in its infancy, my dear, but there is every reason to believe this will work. Your mother may die, but I expect to learn enough to benefit others."

Her mother may die. He said it in the same tone he'd used to tell her about the tropical storm. If there was any other recourse available...but there wasn't. Leland Manning was her mother's only hope.

"I understand."

"Do you? I wonder."

His eyes bore into hers. Brie wanted to cringe away until the brightness of his stare faded.

"I'd like you to reconsider allowing me to test your daughter. Her blood would be quite beneficial...to my research."

Not for any reason whatsoever. Brie now understood completely why people called Manning a vampire behind his back. "I'll think about it."

"Very well." He picked up the vial of her blood and turned away dismissively.

Brie left the laboratory as quickly as possible. She needed someone to talk to about Manning and his research. Someone who would understand. Someone like Elizabeth! She was a certified genius and science was her specialty. Maybe they could meet for dinner or something.

Unfortunately, Maureen had made other plans. With the wedding extravaganza in progress, Brie's input was suddenly vital on every aspect. Thrown into the deep end of the Pierce social whirl, she was only grateful that Becca had arranged a suitable wardrobe for not only Brie, but her mother and Nicole, as well. Items continued to arrive from Boston on a regular basis. In addition to designing the wedding gown and her mother's dress, Becca was also helping in the selection of the other three dresses.

Elizabeth had agreed to act as her maid of honor, Kat would serve as bridesmaid and Nicole would be flower girl, while Kat's little brother, Brandon, would be the ring bearer. Brie was the only one who wasn't surprised when Drew asked Zach, rather than Carey, to serve as his best man. Brie had watched with pleasure as the two brothers had grown close over the past couple of weeks. While Carey agreed to serve as usher, he seemed to be avoiding Drew as much as possible.

Elizabeth wanted to give Brie a wedding shower, but they couldn't fit it into her busy schedule. Maureen insisted Brie and her mother meet with florists, chefs, photographers, musicians and countless others involved in the wedding production. Then there was the visit with Maureen's favorite hair stylist and makeup artist. She'd had Alfred and his assistant brought in from a Boston salon.

Brie had dreaded the event and was tremendously surprised. The stocky Alfred and his shy assistant actually asked questions about her preferences…and he listened. Aware of Drew's desire that she keep her hair long, he came up with a fantastic compromise. He layered the back, leaving the length, but cut the front, taming the unruly curls around her face to add volume and height. The style was not only flattering, but a lot less work to care for. Even Drew seemed pleased.

Not that the two of them had had any time alone together, and when they were, Drew seemed preoccupied.

Curiously, the attacks on Drew had stopped right after the Fourth of July parade. In the past two weeks things had been unusually quiet around town—like the warning silence before a storm. Brie didn't believe it was a coincidence that Mayor Thane had been out of town since then. Drew was still searching for Razz and Dodie, but even Cullen Ryan couldn't find the pair.

Twice she'd glimpsed someone—or something—sliding among the trees in the woods. She made sure the alarm in the cottage was set at all times and warned her mother not to let Nicole out of her sight. But as nothing happened, Brie began to lose some of her caution.

Three days before the wedding, Brie was summoned to the main house. She ignored the shiny new car and set off on foot. She realized her mistake when a rustling sound brought her to a heart-pounding stop. Someone was following her. She'd left her purse and her can of mace at the cottage. Would anyone hear her if she screamed?

The branches parted. David Bryson stepped partially into view. She glimpsed the scar that ran down the side of his face before his long hair fell forward, covering the mark. Brie tried not to stare. He was dressed in black from his dark hair to his black shoes, and he seemed to melt into the shadows.

"David! You scared me! What are you doing here?"

"It isn't safe to walk alone."

"I think you effectively made that point."

"Then let me make another. If you go through with this wedding, watch yourself. The Pierce family isn't loved by everyone."

Fear lifted the hairs on the back of her arms. "What do you mean? Wait, David, don't go!" But he slipped back into the trees as silently as a ghost.

She'd wanted to invite David to the wedding, but the harsh feelings between David and the Pierce clan ran deeper than the death of Tasha. The family had always hated the fact that David had bought the castle, called the Bluffs, out from under them.

So what had David been doing here? He certainly wasn't here by invitation. Should she tell Drew? Not telling him felt disloyal, but she didn't share Drew's hatred, even if David made her uneasy.

Troubled, she hurried along.

"I'm pretty sure I saw Mrs. Pierce in the solarium," a harried worker said distractedly when she asked.

Brie disliked the humid room filled with plants. And not just because Elizabeth had found a body hanging from the rafters in there this past winter. The solarium reminded Brie of a jungle run amok with its earthy smells and trailing vines. She wouldn't have been at all surprised to find a lion stalking her through the place. She was crossing the tiled floor when raised voices made her pause. Geoffrey Pierce and Drew were approaching, locked in what sounded like a bitter personal discussion.

Brie quickly dodged behind an impossibly tall giant fern tree, not wanting to interrupt. But when the two men came to a halt, she found herself trapped, an unwilling listener.

"That is my business and none of your concern," Geoffrey Pierce snarled. "I'm tired of your interest in my activities, Andrew. Your constant hounding is the main reason I moved to the beach house."

"I'm sorry you're upset, but you're leaving me no choice. What is David Bryson's connection to this secret society? I've been hearing some ugly whispers around town—"

"I don't pay attention to rumors and you'd be wise to follow my example."

"Normally I'd agree, however, if this society of yours is involved in something illegal that will bring scandal down on the entire family—"

"Don't you *dare* talk to me about scandal. I'm not the one with little bastards popping up, forcing me into a sham of a marriage with some cheap little waitress."

Brie bit down on a knuckle, feeling ill. Is that what they were saying in town? Drew didn't challenge the assertion. It was Nancy Bell's voice that knifed through the tension. Brie listened to the staccato click of her heels against the tiles as she approached the two men.

"Actually, Dr. Pierce, Drew's popularity around town has never been higher. His engagement to Brianna has only strengthened his position in the working man's community."

"Of course. Wharf rats all love a Cinderella story,"

he sneered. "Even when the prince is only marrying her to save his career."

"Drew! Don't! He's your uncle!"

"I don't care who he is," Drew bit out in a deadly tone of voice Brie had never heard him use before.

"I'm warning you for the last time. Stay out of my business," Geoffrey hissed.

"Drew! No! Let him go," Nancy urged.

Seconds later, Brie glimpsed Geoffrey Pierce outside striding away, his face suffused with bitter anger.

"See if you can get hold of Katherine Ridgemont, Nancy," Drew said tersely. "She goes by the name of Kat most of the time and has a detective agency here in town. I want her to look into this secret society for me."

"But I already have investigators—"

"Your people are being stonewalled and we both know it. We need an insider. Give Kat a call. She was my sister's friend. She'll help if she can. Have you seen Carey?"

"You mean today?"

"Today, yesterday, the day before? He's avoiding my calls."

"Uh, no. I haven't seen him since I came back."

Nancy was lying. Brie had seen the two of them together in the garden only yesterday. They had looked so intimate she hadn't approached. She'd meant to ask Drew if the two of them had developed a personal relationship.

Their voices trailed off as they exited into the garden. Brie heard Maureen's voice outside raised in greeting.

Brie stared around at the unpleasantly hot, humid room, crowded with creeping, sprawling plants, and shuddered.

Pressure filled the air. It had been building for days now. Brie had blamed it on the tropical storm slowly moving up the coast, but now, she wondered. She could almost believe malignant forces were gathering over Moriah's Landing in anticipation of some evil event.

She forced herself to walk, not run, toward the door and freedom from the disturbing room. But the brooding sensation didn't abate in the sunlight. Something evil *was* out of sight, lurking, watching, waiting.

"Brianna, there you are. Your friend Rebecca is a wonder. She's handled those designers with the skill of a diplomat. The rest of your new wardrobe arrived this afternoon and just in time. Did Drew tell you we're having dinner with the governor and his wife tonight?"

Harsh lines bracketed Drew's mouth and eyes. There was still a dark flush to his skin, and the vein in his neck throbbed with anger that hadn't yet found a release.

"I haven't had a chance to mention it, Mother," he muttered. "We haven't even had five minutes to say hello yet today."

She tipped her head, trying to ease his tension. "Hello."

He didn't smile. "Don't let my mother roll over you, Brie. We don't even have to go if you'd rather not."

"Of course you must! I am not trying to roll over anyone, but Andrew, you know your father will be very upset—"

"It's all right, Maureen," Brie said soothingly. "I'd be delighted to meet the governor." And seeing the anger still simmering in Drew's eyes, she added. "And if it will ease Drew's worry, I'll promise not to even mention that ridiculous tax bill the man is proposing."

Drew's expression lightened slowly, but Maureen uttered a tiny sound of dismay. While laughter lines suddenly crinkled around his eyes as he recognized her tease for what it was, his mother chirped away about how certain topics must not be discussed.

"I did warn you, Mother. Brie has a mind of her own. A good mind. The governor could learn a lot from talking with her. This should prove to be a very interesting dinner."

"Good heavens," Maureen whispered.

Brie relaxed as she and Drew shared a private smile. Perhaps, just perhaps, Drew didn't share his uncle's view of their coming marriage.

THE BREWING STORM drew energy into itself until it attained the rating of a full-scale hurricane. Weather reports became the main topic of conversation as slowly the storm drifted closer to the Eastern seaboard.

The morning of the wedding was overcast and more muggy than usual. The tropical smell in the air would have felt right at home inside the Pierce family solarium. Brie and her mother were using a guest bedroom to dress, when they found themselves alone for the first time in days. Her mother looked radiant in a sinfully pretty dress of pale yellow.

"Brie, I'm glad we have a moment. I haven't wanted to say anything because I know how much you love Drew. He's a marvelous father, but I sense you have doubts about this wedding. I just want you to know it's not too late to change your mind."

She had doubts, all right. Major doubts had been chipping away at her sleep and gnawing holes in her stomach. A sham of a wedding, his uncle had called it, and he was right. Drew loved his daughter, but Brie

knew if it hadn't been for Nicole, Drew wouldn't be
waiting with the minister for her right now.

Was she fooling herself that she could make this marriage work for them when half the town seemed to be
aware that Drew didn't love her? But without the Pierce
money, her mother would die. Besides, her daughter
needed her father's love. The bond between them had
taken no time to develop. Nicole adored Drew and he
clearly felt the same. Brie had to make it work, whatever the cost.

"I don't want to change my mind, Mom."

There was a knock on the door and Carey stuck his
head around the corner. "All set? We need to go downstairs. It's time for the mother of the bride to be seated."

Brie felt strangely isolated as Carey led her mother
away. Elizabeth and Kat fussed over the children, waiting for their cue.

"Brianna?"

Startled, she found Yvette standing beside her.

"Yvette! I'm so glad you came." There hadn't been
all that many names on the bride's list. "You need to
walk—"

"I brought you something."

She opened her hand to reveal a pair of delicate crystal earrings. Captivated, Brie lifted one. "They're
lovely."

"I know you aren't into crystals or metaphysical
items, but when I saw these…there is supposed to be
power in certain crystals. These are for you. For luck."

Touched, Brie reached up and removed her grandmother's pearl studs, replacing them with the bits of
glittering glass. "Would you hold on to these for me
until after the ceremony? I don't have anywhere to put
them right now."

Yvette smiled and whisked the pearls into the pocket of her long red skirt. "I won't mislay them."

"I know you won't." She touched the back of Yvette's hand. The woman's features suddenly clouded. Brie had the feeling that Yvette was looking past her, into some vision only she could see.

"Yvette, are you okay?" While the rational part of her knew much of what Yvette did was an act, there was still something almost serenely mystical about the other woman. At moments like this, it was hard not to believe in Yvette's abilities.

"The future changes as each path is chosen. Trust your instincts, Brianna."

Brie nodded. "I am."

DREW STOOD BEFORE THE CROWD. He watched his daughter and Brandon lead the procession. Pamela Dudley caught his eye from her seat in the front row. They shared a smile at the picture the solemn youngsters made. Then Nicole saw him waiting. A broad smile split her face and a tension he hadn't known he felt eased inside him.

"Hi, Daddy! Did I do it right?"

A heart really could swell. Departing from the script, he went forward and gave his daughter a quick hug. "You did it perfectly," he whispered. "You, too, Brandon."

The boy beamed. The children were quickly escorted to their places as Kat and Elizabeth followed them down the makeshift aisle. Then Brie stepped onto the path.

She glowed with a soft radiance. She held her head proudly high, her face utterly serene. The palest of yellow rosebuds and baby's breath adorned her hair, complementing the flowers she carried in her hands. Her dress was elegant in its sheer simplicity.

If Brie had expected fairies in the clearing the other day, he half expected them now. Surely they would be here to watch their queen's marriage to a mere mortal. As their gazes locked, a strange sense of peace settled over him. He wasn't aware he'd moved from his brother's side until he'd taken her hand and led her the rest of the way.

"Daddy, you were supposed to wait over there," his daughter scolded.

"Sorry, sweetheart, I forgot."

"That's okay."

Everyone smiled as they joined the minister under the trellis of roses and ivy. Everyone except Carey. Drew filed that puzzle away for later. His attention centered on Brie, the minister, and vow he was about to make.

THEY WERE MARRIED. The fact seemed as unreal as the people swirling around Brie. Her feet hurt and her face was stiff from smiling. Famous people, from politicians, to the movers and shakers in the business world, to some of the biggest names in the entertainment industry had attended her wedding. Thankfully, Drew hadn't left her side—until she finally escaped to the blissful solitude of the bathroom. Her image displayed no sign of the exhaustion tugging at her. She wandered back outside reluctantly, pleased to find Elizabeth and Kat standing nearby chatting with Becca. These were her guests. Her friends.

"Brie, you look like you need something to drink. Here."

Brie accepted the glass of sparkling water Elizabeth handed her with a grateful smile.

"You're a mind reader. I was dying of thirst."

"The wedding was perfect."

"Do you think so?"

"Absolutely, though I think you were upstaged by your daughter. She melted every heart in the yard when she called Drew Daddy."

"They were adorable," Claire agreed, drifting over to join them.

Brie hugged her friend tightly, happy to see Claire finally looking so well after all this time. "I am so glad you came today."

"Me, too." She glanced around nervously at the huge crowd of people. "You look like a princess, Brie."

"Thanks to Becca," she agreed, smiling at the woman who stood on the fringe of their circle. "Come over and join us."

Kat snagged a passing waiter carrying a tray of champagne. "We need these. I want to propose a toast."

The others accepted glasses of the wildly expensive vintage and waited.

"To old friends and new ones," Kat said, including Becca with a warm smile. "May the future draw us close together once more."

"Hear, hear," Elizabeth agreed.

"And to friends who are gone, but never forgotten," Claire added shyly.

Their thoughts turned to Tasha as Claire had intended. The five of them clinked glasses and drank a pledge to deepen the bond they had forged. Through a gap in the crowd Brie found Drew watching, a smile of approval lighting his eyes.

She touched an earring lightly and thought Yvette might have been right. There might indeed be something of power in these tiny glass shards. Maybe this wasn't a perfect marriage, but it didn't have to be a sham. They liked each other and there was no denying their powerful chemistry. It would be enough. She would make it be enough.

Drew turned away from Brie reluctantly. His wife, he thought in satisfaction, would be there later. Right now he was determined not to let Carey elude him again. "We need to talk, friend."

"Later."

"You've been saying that for two weeks."

"You've been busy for two weeks."

Carey wouldn't meet his eyes. "Not that busy. You're avoiding me. Are the rumors true?"

"Which rumors? This town has so many it's hard to keep track."

"Carey, I know you're in trouble. Let me help."

To his shock, Carey's expression turned bitter. "Good old Drew, always there with a hand for a friend. Did it ever occur to you that I might actually be able to solve my own problems? You want to play big brother, go find Zach."

"Excuse me, Carey," William Pierce interrupted, totally unaware of the undercurrent. "Senator LaFleur needs to speak with Drew before he has to leave. Will you excuse us?"

"Gladly."

Drew reluctantly allowed himself to be led over to a group of politicians and their wives. Even as he smiled and chatted, he wondered at Carey's bitterness. Drew hated the suspicion crawling around in his head. But he couldn't shake it loose. What if Carey had known he was about to be disinherited? What if he'd conspired with Ursula Manning to pretend she'd been kidnapped to gain the ransom money?

Carey was a playboy. Drew didn't want to believe he was a thief.

With absolutely no warning, a woman's shrill scream sent him spinning toward Brie.

Chapter Twelve

Brie reached for Claire as the glass slipped from her fingers, showering them all with champagne.

"No, no, no, no!"

With shocking strength, she tore from Brie's grasp. Claire raced blindly toward the solarium, her face a rictus mask of terror. Dogs were barking furiously.

Brie glanced over her shoulder. Her gaze landed on David Bryson. Dressed in black as always, he stood beside a large ornamental shrub watching Security chase two fleeing figures. She was absolutely certain David wasn't on the guest list, but she couldn't worry about his presence right now. She hurried after Claire. By the time she reached her friend, Claire was curled tightly in a ball behind the tall fern tree, rocking and weeping silently. Elizabeth dropped to the floor beside her, keeping her voice soft and gentle as she murmured to Claire and stroked her rigid body.

"What happened?" Drew asked at Brie's side.

"I don't know." Her own cheeks were damp with tears. She hadn't even known she was crying. "We were just talking. Suddenly she started screaming."

Cullen began clearing the room and Brie leaned into

Drew gratefully as he slid an arm around her shoulders. "He's here, isn't he? The person who hurt her?"

"Shh." Drew glanced around quickly to be sure no one had overheard. "We don't know that. She's been ill a long time, Brie. Maybe someone or something reminded her of the kidnapping. You told me yourself you weren't sure Claire could handle being in such a large group."

"But her reaction—"

"Ambulance is on the way," Kat said, walking over to them. Jonah Ries had an arm wrapped possessively around Kat's waist, but his features were grim.

"Security nabbed two men who came in over the wall with an arsenal of smoke bombs, spray paint, knives—"

"Razz and Dodie," Brie said immediately.

"I'll wring their necks," Drew promised.

She gripped his arm. Her eyes went to Claire, who lay rigid and unmoving in Elizabeth's arms. "You don't think…?"

Cullen joined them and followed her gaze. A hard, professional mask settled over his features. "I'll find out what those two were doing here." His jaw set. "You'll press charges?"

"Absolutely," Drew agreed.

"Besides Razz and Dodie, do any of you know who Claire was looking at right before she screamed?"

Kat stepped forward. "I was facing the same direction. There were a number of people in our direct line of sight. Anton Pierce was talking with Anita Lovett, the movie star, and her husband. Brie's mother, Nicole and Brandon, Zach and Em were also standing there. Carey Eldrich and Nancy Bell were having a conversation with a man I didn't recognize. And Leland Manning, Geoffrey Pierce, Mayor Thane, his aide and two other men I didn't recognize were clustered together to the right of them.''

''You saw all this?'' Cullen asked in amazement.

''I was sort of keeping an eye on the situation.'' She shrugged. ''You know, in case Dr. Manning had learned that Carey was having an affair with his wife. I didn't want any trouble.''

Brie's gaze returned to Claire. Her friend's pain was horrible to witness. Brie felt so cold she wondered if she would ever feel warm again.

FULL DARK DESCENDED before Brie entered Drew's ''cottage.'' She was too tired to do more than note it was a mirror image of the one she'd been sharing with her mother.

''Make yourself at home,'' Drew told her. ''Staff should have put your wardrobe in the master bedroom down that hall. I want to have a word with the security man outside, then I'll be right in.''

Since Razz and Dodie had been captured, there could only be one reason for the strong security measures being taken to guard the cottages tonight. Drew didn't think the danger was over.

She made her way down the hall, feeling numb all over. Two steps into the master bedroom she halted. A small crystal lamp glowed softly. The bed had been turned down. An exquisite red rose and a foil-wrapped square of expensive chocolate lay on each pillow. A bottle of champagne sat chilling in a crystal ice bucket on a stand beside the bed. Two fluted crystal glasses rested on the nightstand. The scent of roses wafted from a large vase on the mahogany dresser, spilling over with the deep red blooms. Soft music played from invisible speakers. And a filmy blue peignoir she'd never seen before had been laid out at the foot of the bed.

"Brie? Is something—" Drew came to a stop at her back, surveying the scene "—wrong?" He uttered a whispered oath. He walked over and lifted the filmy bit of nylon and lace. Brie saw he'd already removed his tie and unbuttoned the top three buttons on his shirt. He looked unbearably sexy. "Nice. But hardly subtle."

"Are you saying this wasn't your doing?"

Ruefully, he shook his head. "Probably I should have thought to have champagne waiting, but it never occurred to me."

"Then who?"

Drew shrugged. "My mother?"

"Your mother!"

He looked down at the peignoir and shook his head. "You're right. This isn't exactly her style, is it?" He dropped the gown onto the bed and began shrugging out of the tuxedo jacket.

Brie inhaled a shaky breath, not certain what to do or where to look. Was he planning to get undressed right here in front of her? Her gaze landed on two large suitcases. "Drew?"

"It's okay. I had them packed for our honeymoon. You're still pretty rocky, aren't you? It's been a long day."

A rushing sound seemed to fill her head. "What honeymoon? We aren't going on a honeymoon."

"Well, not now we aren't," he said wryly. He raked his fingers through his hair. "Our flight to Bermuda was canceled this evening. Seems that storm is playing havoc with air travel."

"You planned a honeymoon?"

"That was supposed to be *my* surprise. So, surprise."

His wry smile changed to concern and he crossed to her. "Hey, it was supposed to be a surprise, not a shock. A honeymoon is traditional after a wedding, you know."

He'd been planning a honeymoon.

Of course he had. Those five-hundred-plus guests who witnessed their "quiet" garden wedding would expect no less. She was the only one who'd given the idea no thought.

Because she hadn't let herself think beyond the wedding itself.

"I think...I'm too tired to think."

He stroked her shoulder with a tenderness that made her want to cry. "I can see that. Why don't you change out of your dress?"

"Into that?" she asked, nodding at the peignoir.

His eyes glittered. "Well, I certainly wouldn't mind, but I warn you, if you put that on you won't be wearing it for long."

Maybe she hadn't let herself think past the wedding itself, but now that's all she could think about. This was her wedding night—and Drew was flirting with her, the way he had that day at Threads. Except now there was a hungry edge to the flirting. No more barriers. They were man and wife.

He'd planned on a honeymoon.

A tingling fire hummed its way along every nerve cell. She was exquisitely, painfully aware of Drew. His scent. The way his chest filled that shirt. The knowledge that his mouth had the power to draw the most elemental response from her.

"Come here, Mrs. Pierce."

The husky timbre of his order weakened her knees,

threatening her equilibrium. Had she moved or was it him? He lifted her chin with his knuckle.

"I've been horribly remiss today," he said softly. "I never once told you what an incredibly lovely bride you made."

He reached for the flowers in her hair, removing them one by one, dropping them heedlessly to the floor. All, save the last one. He trailed the velvety, fragrant petals down the side of her face, brushing her lips, running it down her neck, across her breasts and the nipples straining behind the fabric of her dress. Then he let it fall as well. Pulling her gently forward, his fingers threaded through her hair, discovering sensitive nerves she hadn't even known existed. Her heart slammed against her ribs as he lowered his head to inhale the scent of her hair.

"Don't ever change your shampoo."

Her body quivered in uncontrollable excitement.

"All day I watched you glide around in this simple, sensual gown, and I counted the minutes until I could turn it into an ivory pool at your feet," he murmured.

Mesmerized by his tender expression far more than his words, she stood still while his arms slid around her neck, his fingers seeking the hidden zipper at her back. His lips nibbled at her throat, the curve of her cheek, skimming over lips that craved the taste of him.

"Ah, here we go."

He turned her around before she knew what he meant to do. Air brushed the skin of her back as he inched the zipper downward, stopping to plant tiny kisses along the way against her spine. The sensation was wildly erotic. She couldn't control the trembling that had taken hold of her.

"Drew!"

"Shh. Hold still, I'm not finished yet."

"Hold still? I can barely stand up."

Drew chuckled softly. He slid an arm beneath her breasts to support her. "I won't let you fall."

And her nipples puckered, achingly aware of that arm so tantalizingly close. The dress slithered over her hips, spilling over the carpeting.

"A garter! I love surprises."

Before she could tell him the sexy undergarments had been Becca's idea of a surprise, he placed a kiss at the base of her spine, between the bottom of her lacy garter and above the low line of her high-cut satin panties. Her belly quivered. Her buttocks tightened, and he stood, pulling her back against his body until she could feel the throbbing pulse of his arousal right through his slacks as it pressed against her bottom.

"You feel so good. Turn around and let me see you."

Heat bathed her body as the sensual rhythm of his words stirred the torrent of suppressed desire. Embarrassed, yet stimulated by his command, she did as he asked, nearly falling as her high heels tangled in the dress. Drew steadied her, pulling the material from under her feet, pausing to kiss the calf of her leg right through her sheer nylons.

Ripples of anticipation skimmed over her. She spread her fingers through the silky strands of his hair as she clutched his head, needing support just to stand. The hot, moist breath of his mouth against her panties weakened her knees so much she was forced to grab his shoulders to hold herself upright. He deliberately brushed the length of her body as he stood, those brilliant blue eyes smoldering with desire.

"Take them off for me."

"Wh-what?"

He crushed her mouth under his. She melted into his

fierce embrace, yielding to the hot, wet kiss that went on and on, destroying all possibility of rational thought. She wanted him. She had always wanted him.

"Your stockings," he murmured against her ear, pausing to lick the lobe, sending her earring swinging. "I want to watch you peel them from your legs."

Embarrassment was no match for the feverish longing swirling inside her. He stepped back. Breathless, intensely conscious of him, she raised her leg, resting it against the bed. His bright blue eyes watched her with a ravenous fascination that was somehow empowering. He wanted her—every bit as much as she wanted him. This would be no mindless coupling in the sand. Not even a frenzied coupling in the woods. This was seduction. Slow, simmering seduction that he intended to prolong until neither of them could take the teasing any longer.

Brie's lips curved. She might not have any experience in seduction, but she suspected experience wasn't necessary. Her fingers shook only a little as she released the first garter. Slowly, she stroked the nylon down the length of her leg, watching him watch her.

Drew finished unbuttoning his shirt, never once lifting his gaze from her. She was pleased to see his fingers weren't all that steady, either. She removed the shoe and stocking together. Then she kicked off the other shoe, and repeated the process as he shrugged out of his shirt and cummerbund.

She undid the snaps holding up the garter as his hands went to his waistband. The sound of his zipper was electrifying. Her stomach fluttered madly as he kicked off his shoes and lowered his pants. He was fully, vibrantly aroused.

"I wanted to take my time, but—"

"We've wasted enough time."

"Yes."

And he toppled her onto the bed, following her down with a greedy longing that set her soul ablaze. Her bra and panties disappeared under the magic of his mouth and fingers. Never had her body felt so vibrantly alive, so exquisitely tuned. She whimpered softly, and Drew smiled, prolonging the moment until neither of them could stand the waiting another second. She couldn't look away from his glittering eyes as he claimed her body, just as he'd claimed her heart. She nearly blurted out the words of love that filled her mind. It was a very long time before either one of them stirred after the universe exploded and they fell over the edge of the world.

Replete in a way he had never felt before, Drew pulled back the covers, switched off the light and tugged her close to his sweat-slicked side. Her head rested against his shoulder. Her hair tickled his nose. He hadn't needed the tightness of her body to tell him that her earlier reputation was totally unfounded. Her enthusiastic but untutored response to his lovemaking made him wonder if she'd had any lovers at all since that night on the beach. Primitive satisfaction washed over him.

"You are the most beautiful woman I have ever seen."

"And you've seen so many."

"Does it bother you that there were other women in my life?"

"In your life, no. In your bed, of course."

That candidly refreshing honesty of hers. It never ceased to amaze him.

"I'm incredibly selfish about some things, Drew. I want to be the only one."

"You are," he promised. "We took a vow. It's one I mean to honor, Brie." Tension eased slowly from her body. He stroked her cheek with his fingertips. "Besides, having a wildcat in my bed is exhausting. Where would I find the energy to look elsewhere?"

She rolled over to face him and her breasts pushed temptingly against his arm. "A wildcat?"

"Hmm." He kissed the tip of her nose. "A beautiful, fierce, sexy wildcat. And she's finally all mine."

Even in the dark, he saw something wistful in her expression, but she settled back against him, curling her body against his. "I should get up and take a shower."

"We'll take one together—in a little while."

For a long time, neither of them moved. He thought she'd fallen asleep when she spoke, her voice thick with the tiredness that weighed on him as well.

"Do you think Claire will remember?"

He forced himself to relax. "Maybe."

"The last time she got this upset was when Elizabeth, Kat and I went to the sanitarium. We left there feeling terrible for causing her such pain, but right after that she began to improve. It scares me to think that monster might have been one of our guests."

He tightened his arm around her. The thought scared him, as well. "Go to sleep."

Her voice relaxed along with her body. "I'm glad you posted guards. If anything happened to Nicole or my mother…"

"Nothing will happen to them," he said fiercely.

"I know." She yawed and snuggled closer. "You'll protect us."

And her complete faith left him staring at the ceiling long after she drifted into a peaceful, deep sleep.

CAREY KNEW WHAT EVERYONE was thinking. Cullen Ryan had questioned him until he'd wanted to hit something. How could anyone believe him capable of torturing a woman? Carey loved women. His idea of torture was to bring them to the peak of satisfaction over and over again. The idea that he might have hurt Ursula was unthinkable. Worse was the way they suggested he might have had something to do with what happened to Claire. Hell, he'd been a kid when she was kidnapped.

Okay, so he'd known her. He'd even liked her. There had been something fascinating about her—in an innocent little-lamb sort of way. But Carey had never been stupid. He preferred women like Ursula and Nancy. Beautiful women who knew the score and didn't demand things like permanence or wedding rings.

But he could feel a noose closing around his neck. He had a feeling they'd like to take him to the town green and hang him like they had old McFarland Leary.

He left the police station and walked to where he'd parked his car. Reaching for his keys, he glimpsed a familiar figure ghosting past like an evil shadow. He crouched beside the car and watched intently. Interesting. Now what was he doing out here at this hour?

Carey knew if he was going to keep from getting arrested, he would have to discover who had murdered Ursula himself. He couldn't rely on the police. And right there went someone with his own motive for her murder. Carey trailed in the figure's wake.

He thought about the job Nancy had helped him find in Boston. Nancy was special. She saw right through his easygoing pretense. She got him to talk about things he never had with anyone else. It was Nancy who suggested he come to Boston and talk to some people she knew. Work had never interested him before, but this was different. Exciting. Challenging. Certainly better than selling advertising for the family paper.

The figure he was following jerked to a stop and cast a nervous look around. Carey prayed he was deep enough into the building's shadows that he couldn't be seen. Waterfront Avenue was ominously dark and silent. Had he given himself away? Maybe the man had heard his footfalls against the worn cobblestones. He'd have to be more careful. He should allow more space between them. He wished there had been time to change clothing. Sneaking around in a tuxedo and dress shoes was stupid, but there hadn't been much choice. He felt foolish as he glanced behind him, checking the street at his back.

Nothing stirred.

He turned back and his quarry had vanished. Probably gone inside the strip club on the corner. Could he follow without being spotted? He hurried forward.

Something came out of the darkness as he passed the tattoo parlor, smashing against his skull with stunning force. Carey staggered back. The second blow split the skin. Blood trickled down his face. His vision blurred. He lurched against the building. Something smashed his knee and Carey fell, sliding down the jagged brick facade.

His head reeled with pain. He couldn't seem to make his limbs obey. Something sharp plunged into the side of his neck. He felt the burn and sting even as he tried to fight against the bite of the needle. Carey tried to protest, but his mouth wouldn't cooperate. He couldn't focus on the face over his.

"On your feet, Mr. Eldrich. The kneecap isn't broken—yet. We're going to take a ride, you and I. I have a nice black hearse waiting. And it just so happens I have an empty coffin inside."

His mind screamed in horror, but the screams never left his throat.

Chapter Thirteen

Only half-awake, Drew rolled over, reaching for Brie, as had become his habit over the past two days. But he found only empty blankets. Instantly, his eyes opened. She stood by the window watching the rain. Her hair was a disheveled flame of color against the white satin drapes. She'd pulled on one of his shirts in lieu of a robe. He made a mental note to throw out any robes she owned. He wondered if he would ever tire of looking at her. His wife.

"Brie?"

She turned, letting the drape fall back into place. "The storm's moving."

"It's supposed to hit South Carolina today."

"I don't think so. I think it's coming here."

He patted the bed at his side. She glided over but didn't sit down.

"Even if it does, Moriah's Landing has withstood any number of hurricanes. We'll be okay."

She shook her head. "Don't you feel it? There's a pressure in the air, like something bad waiting to happen."

Drew slid out of the bed and pulled her into his arms. She shivered. "I knew you didn't like storms, but I didn't know they bothered you this much. Let's go take a shower and warm you up."

She lifted her face with a trace of humor. "I don't think my body could survive another shower with you. My bones are still melted from the last one." But anticipation flickered in her eyes. It was noon before they got around to getting dressed.

"Do you realize we haven't left this house since the wedding?"

"Hmm. Shall we go for a record?"

"You're all talk."

"Not *all* talk."

"I need to be sure Nicole and my mother are okay."

"You talked to them yesterday."

"But I haven't seen them."

"Ah, this is a visual need. Okay. I miss the little imp, too—and I don't mean her cat. Let's go over and see if they want to do lunch and take in a movie. It's too wet to do much else."

"We should call first."

"We can be there in the same amount of time. You really are worried, aren't you?"

"Not about them. I know they're okay."

"The storm?"

"It's my talent. You charm people and I sense storms. And you can stop looking at me like that. My ancestor was hung because she could predict the weather."

"Little witch. You bewitched me the first day I saw you."

She made a face. "I was ten. You looked right through me when we were introduced."

"Blinded by your beauty."

"Uh-huh. Drew, if you don't stop kissing me, we're never going to leave."

"What a great idea!"

Laughing, she pulled away. "Put your shoes on."

"Spoilsport."

The telephone rang as she was reaching for the doorknob. With an apologetic look, Drew lifted the receiver.

"Drew? Cullen Ryan. Am I catching you at a bad time?"

"If this had been a bad time, I wouldn't have bothered answering. Brie and I were just going out the door. What's up?"

"Have you seen Carey Eldrich?"

"Not since the wedding."

"Any idea where I might find him?"

"I gather you tried his place?" Brie came to stand at his side. Reflexively, he put an arm around her and pulled her against him.

"And the newspaper," Cullen was saying, "and his family, and everyone else I can think of. He seems to have disappeared."

"Knowing Carey, he's probably with someone he met at the wedding."

Brie frowned.

"Hadn't thought of that. Okay, I'll keep checking, but if you see him, tell him I want to talk to him again."

"Cullen, you don't really think Carey had anything to do with Claire or Ursula's abductions do you?"

Brie inhaled sharply.

"Because you're wasting your time. Carey would never hurt a woman. I know the man. I'd stake my life on it."

There was a pause before Cullen said quietly,

"Would you stake Brie's life on it? If you see him, tell him to give me a call."

Ryan disconnected. Drew was much slower to replace the receiver.

"You're right," Brie said forcefully. "Carey would never hurt anyone."

Drew might not be sensitive to storms, but it didn't take a witch to feel the oppression hanging over this town. "Let's go see our daughter."

But after arriving at the main house, they learned Maureen had taken Pamela and Nicole shopping for the day.

"Shopping for what? Your mother already bought us enough new clothing to last a lifetime."

"That bothers you, doesn't it?"

Brie nodded. "I don't like taking charity. I like to earn my own way."

"You married a very stubborn woman," Anton Pierce said, coming down the hall. Drew felt Brie's tension as they turned to greet his grandfather.

"Do you know this young woman has paid back nearly all of the money I gave her to keep her away from you four years ago?"

Brie inhaled sharply and Drew slid a protective arm around her waist. "I'm not a bit surprised."

She tried to wriggle free, but Drew wouldn't let her. His grandfather smiled.

"I was. I'm not usually such a bad judge of character. I was wrong about you, girl."

"Thank you. But I'm afraid the next few installments are going to be late," she told his grandfather. "Drew got me fired."

"I would hope so," Anton sniffed.

"I didn't realize you liked your job so much," Drew

said, kissing the top of her head just to watch her squirm. "If waiting tables means that much to you, I'm sure I can get them to take you back."

"Andrew!" his grandfather reprimanded.

But Brie looked up at him, the light of battle shining in her bright green eyes. "Not a bad idea. Maybe I can get them to hire you on as a busboy," she said tartly. "You know, in case your bid for mayor fails."

Drew laughed out loud. His grandfather scowled. "You have a perverted sense of humor, young lady."

"Thank you."

"We're going out to grab a bite to eat," Drew told him. "Would you care to join us?"

"No, thank you. Your father and I have a meeting with some people this afternoon."

"All right. We'll see you later, then."

"I shouldn't tease your grandfather like that," Brie said after he disappeared into his office.

"On the contrary. He likes it. He likes you."

Brie made a face. "How can you tell?"

"Years of experience."

"Uh-huh. Drew, would you mind if we stop and see Claire?"

"Good idea. We'll grab something at the diner and head over to her place afterward."

"The diner?"

"Wouldn't you like to see what it's like from the other side of the counter?"

Nancy called down to them from the landing of the highly polished oak staircase. "May I speak with you for a moment?"

"Hi, Nancy. I thought you went back to Boston yesterday."

"No, I, uh, had a change of plans." She hurried down

to the foyer. "Have you, uh, seen or heard from Carey by any chance? I mean since the wedding?"

It wasn't like Nancy to hesitate or not meet his eyes. "You're the second person to ask me that this morning."

Her head came up sharply. "Who else is looking for him?"

"Cullen Ryan."

Her features paled. Carey had been taken with Nancy from the start. He should have known his friend would put moves on her. "Don't tell me you fell for the Eldrich charm, too."

"It isn't like that." She raised her head defiantly. "I'm not naive, Andrew. Carey is fun, intelligent and wasting his life because he lacks focus. But now that he's stopped trying to measure up to you, he's changing. He's got a good job in Boston. One that will challenge him. It will be good for him to be away from his family and their pressure to be more like you."

"His family's been holding me up as some sort of model?"

"Surely you knew. But it doesn't matter. He doesn't care that his family cut him off. He's ready to make big changes in his life, but the police are hounding him because of that affair with Ursula. You know he didn't harm anyone. I'm really worried. I think something's happened to him."

"Ryan's a good cop, Nancy. He's not going to railroad anyone. The cops just want to know where he got the money to pay off his debts all of a sudden."

"I loaned him the money. I know what you're thinking, but he couldn't go to you. It would have destroyed his pride. I made him a business offer. He was reluctant at first, but when he saw the possibilities, he decided to accept a chance to start over. He was supposed to meet me after the police let him go the other night, but he never came. His tuxedo is missing and no one has seen him since he left the police station.''

Drew's stomach lurched. ''Where have you looked?''

''Everywhere I can think of. Something's wrong. We were supposed to drive back to Boston together yesterday. He has a meeting tomorrow morning.''

The housekeeper appeared in the library doorway. ''Excuse me, Mrs. Pierce. There's a telephone call for you. Your mother's doctor?''

It took Brie a second to realize *she* was the Mrs. Pierce being addressed. ''Oh.''

''Take it in the library,'' Drew said. ''Will you show her, May?''

''Certainly. This way, Mrs. Pierce.''

Brie followed the gaunt woman into a room whose dark, richly paneled walls were filled to the ceiling with shelves of books. This was a genuine library, she realized.

''The telephone is at that desk, Mrs. Pierce.''

''Thank you.'' She skirted the grand piano and crossed to the ornate writing desk. ''Hello? Dr. Thornton?''

There was a momentary pause. The tone came out sharp and stiff. ''This is Dr. Manning.''

''Oh. I'm sorry. I assumed—'' Flustered, Brie forced herself to calm down. ''Dr. Manning, what can I do for you?''

''I called to discuss a schedule so we may begin your mother's treatments. I assume she still wishes to be a test case?''

Something visceral slithered up her spine. Brie

gripped the receiver tightly. "She's not here right now."

"We should begin immediately. I agreed to wait until after your wedding, but we really must proceed now if this treatment is to be effective. Each day we delay increases the odds against a successful test case."

Fear rooted in her mind. A test case. As if her mother wasn't a human being at all. "I'll ask her to call you this afternoon as soon as she returns."

"Do that."

The click was as abrupt as his tone. Leland Manning was a brilliant geneticist and scientist. But where was the empathy? The concern for his patient? Was she making a horrible mistake to entrust her mother to such a chilling man?

Raised voices came from the hall. Drew and his uncle were at each other again. She hurried out in time to see Geoffrey Pierce storm toward the back of the house. Nancy was gone.

"What happened?"

Drew's face was surprisingly composed. "I'm not sure. I asked him if he'd seen Carey. He started yelling, telling me to stay out of his business."

"That doesn't make any sense."

"I know."

"Where did Nancy go?" she asked as they ran back to the car.

"She had some business to attend to."

"Do you really mean to go to the diner?"

"Is there a better place in town for gossip?"

"One of the bars?"

"I am not taking you into some dingy bar to be drooled over by a bunch of drunks."

"Rider and Jake might take umbrage with that description."

"I doubt it. You'll notice they have the good sense to come to the diner for food."

"Point taken."

IT FELT WEIRD TO HAVE LOIS wait on her inside the familiar diner.

"Fantastic wedding, you two. I had such a good time. What a shame about poor little Claire Cavendish. I'm glad Cullen arrested those two little vandals. I hope he throws away the key."

"You think Claire was upset because of Razz and Dodie?"

"Well, sure. They upset a lot of people."

While the diner wasn't crowded at this hour, several patrons made it a point to stop by their booth to say hello and chat for a few minutes. Brie noticed the people were treating Drew like one of the them. Nancy had been right, marriage to Brie had enhanced Drew's status on the wharf side of town.

When Drew excused himself to use the rest room, Brie saw Yvette Castor enter the diner. The fortune-teller glanced around and headed straight for her booth. Her gaudy jewelry clanked noisily as she leaned over the table, but it was her anxious expression that captured Brie's full attention.

"I know you're a nonbeliever, Brianna, but I must warn you."

A breeze swept over her skin.

"The signs are murky and more twisted than normal. There are so many variables, but you must not let down your guard. Someone lurks in the shadows, Brianna."

Big J. from the tattoo parlor stuck his head in the

front door and yelled to Yvette. "Hey, Madam Fleury, you got a customer." Yvette waved acknowledgement. She touched the crystal earrings Brie wore again this morning. "They won't be enough." Looking up as Drew approached, she turned to him. "Don't let her go anywhere alone." And Yvette was gone in a swirl of color and a clanking of jewelry.

"What was that all about?" Drew asked.

"I'm not sure. Yvette isn't usually this strange, but she seems to think I'm in some sort of danger."

Drew opened his wallet and withdrew several bills. "Let's go."

Brie stood immediately. She, too, felt the need for action. "So did we learn anything?"

"Yeah. The diner still makes great pie."

"Very funny. I meant about Carey."

"No one has seen him since he left the police station."

"So where are we going?"

"To look for his car."

"His car?"

Drew smiled wryly. "He brought mine back right before the wedding."

"Oh. Well, surely you don't think something happened to him at a police station?"

Drew pointed to a cherry-red sports car parked in the lot behind the newspaper building two doors down from the police station. "Now I do. That's Carey's car."

DETECTIVE RYAN WASN'T THERE when they went to let him know about the discovery, but Chief Redfern himself bustled over to take the information. Drew kept his dislike well concealed.

Their moods were as dark as the sky overhead when

they drove to Claire's house. Luck wasn't with them there, either. Claire and Rebecca Smith had gone off together and Claire's brother had no idea when they'd be back.

"I'd say it's a good sign if she's out doing things with Becca," Drew said. Brie nodded, but he could tell she was still worried.

The wind picked up, making the rain seem heavier than before. The air was decidedly unpleasant. Drew wondered if Brie might be right about the storm. At the compound, they discovered Pamela had returned to the guest cottage due to a vicious headache.

"Let me call Dr. Thornton, Mom."

"I already did. He's going to stop by in a little while."

"Oh. Well how about if we take Nicole with us so you can lie down?"

"That would be nice."

Brie cast him a worried look. Drew shared her concern. Pamela didn't look well at all.

"We'll keep Nicole and the cats with us tonight. Do you want me to take Fitzwiggy as well?"

"No, dear. Fitz is good company."

"All right. We'll lock up when we leave."

Drew helped gather up litter pans, cat toys and scratching posts while Brie and Nicole packed her toys and clothing and loaded them into the car Drew had given her.

Until today, when Nancy had explained why Carey hadn't come to him for a loan, Drew hadn't understood what it cost Brie's pride to accept his gift of the car, but she hadn't even argued over the substantial checking account he had opened in her name because she needed the money to pay for her mother's treatments.

But was that the only reason she'd married him? The idea lay bitter in his mind.

The telephone was ringing when he carried the last item inside. The voice on the other end sounded muffled, as if the person were covering the mouthpiece.

"Carey Eldrich is in danger."

"Who is this?"

"If you want to help, be at the wharf at seven-thirty. Come alone."

A click ended the call.

"Who was that?"

Drew repeated the conversation.

"Call Cullen," she demanded.

"The voice said to come alone."

"You aren't—"

"Of course not, but Ryan wasn't in the office, remember?"

"I have their home number."

Drew shook his head. "I'm not leaving you and Nicole here alone." The fortune-teller's warning suddenly loomed in his head. "Not even for Carey. What if it was a ruse to get me away so someone could get at you?"

"What if it was a ruse to get you alone?" She reached for the telephone. "I'm calling Elizabeth. I wanted to talk to her anyhow."

The phone rang four times. Brie was about to hang up when Elizabeth answered breathlessly. Brie knew immediately that her friend was distracted and excited over something. She'd probably caught her in the middle of an experiment.

"Elizabeth, it's Brie. I'm sorry to bother you, but we need your help." She could almost see her friend shifting priorities. "Is Cullen there?"

"No, but I'm expecting him home any minute."

"Would you mind if we came over for a few minutes? Drew just got an anonymous call about Carey. We think it may be a trap."

"Come over. We'll be here waiting."

"Thanks Elizabeth." She hung up and looked at Drew. "Okay?"

"Let's go."

But it wasn't quite that simple. Nicole refused to leave Little Imp. Even Max acted agitated as he butted against Brie's legs.

"What's gotten into him? Maybe it's all this moving around. I'll give them a treat while you put Nicole in her car seat."

"Sure. You get the easy job." But Drew smiled and lifted his daughter. "We're going see Elizabeth, Nicole. We can't take the cats over there, but we're coming right back."

Nicole was not pacified. Brie had never seen her daughter throw such a tantrum. And the cats wouldn't come near the offered treat. The minute Drew opened the front door, Max tried to escape. In the end, they loaded the cats back into carriers and took them, as well.

"The score is daughter and cats one, parents zip. I hope this isn't an omen," Drew said.

"Very funny. Do you know where we're going?"

"I'll follow you. Drive carefully. With all this rain we're bound to see flash flooding pretty soon."

Brie nodded. Max and Imp loudly protested their confinement and her normally happy daughter was in a mood nearly as bad. It was not a happy group that landed on Elizabeth and Cullen's doorstep a few minutes later. Brie was thankful to see Elizabeth's brother, Brandon, was visiting, which immediately improved her daughter's mood.

While the men talked, the women got the children settled in front of the television with pizza and a movie.

"We're interrupting your dinner," Brie said apologetically.

"No, you aren't. I have to teach a class at seven-thirty. I was just feeding Brandon before I ran him home. We'll eat later. Would you like something?"

"No, thanks."

"Tell me what's going on."

Brie heard Cullen on the phone in the other room. Quickly she summarized what she knew. "Drew didn't want me to stay alone, but as soon as the men leave, I'll head back to the compound."

"You're welcome to wait here, though the Pierce estate is like a fortress."

"One made of Swiss cheese, maybe."

"Dodie and Razz got inside, but Security caught them."

"They didn't catch David Bryson. He was in the woods the other day and he even came to the wedding."

"You're kidding! Really?"

"Oh, my God, Elizabeth. I just realized. David was there when Security was chasing Razz and Dodie. What if he's the one Claire was looking at when she had her breakdown?"

"Who was Claire looking at?" Cullen asked, striding into the room.

Brie stared at the men. "David Bryson. I just remembered he was watching Security chase Razz and Dodie."

"Bryson was at our wedding?"

Brie nodded, breathing as if she'd just run a mile. "I forgot in all the commotion."

Drew exchanged dark looks with Cullen. He turned to her with a fierce expression. "You stay with Elizabeth until we get back, do you understand?"

"Drew's right," Cullen interjected. "We'll be back as soon as we can." He gave his wife a quick kiss on the lips. "Stay out of trouble, all right?"

"You know me."

"That's the problem. Come on, Drew."

Drew made no move to kiss her as Cullen had done with Elizabeth. Brie pushed her hurt aside as he strode ahead of Cullen and out the door. Drew had a right to be upset. He considered David his enemy and she hadn't told him how David had been spying on him. She swallowed hard. Her friend laid a comforting hand on her shoulder.

"Brie, I can't cancel class at this hour. I'm afraid you and Nicole will have to come and sit in."

"No offense, but I don't think so."

"But you promised Drew."

"No, he gave me an order. I didn't agree to obey. He forgot I've got the cats in the car. But before I go I wanted to talk to you about something."

Brie told Elizabeth about Leland Manning's experimental procedure and her second thoughts about the whole thing.

"So am I putting my mother at risk in your opinion?"

"Yes! Under no circumstances let your mother go to Manning. My God, what you've told me—it's all starting to fit! Come on back to my lab."

"You have a lab?"

"Actually, it's a spare bedroom Cullen converted for

me when we rented this house. He thinks I've been wasting my time, but I've been doing some research into the recent serial killings here in Moriah's Landing."

"Do you mean the women whose bodies were left for you to find? But, Cullen caught the killer."

"But it bothered me that he could never find a substantial connection among any of the women. Not this time, and not twenty years ago when there was a whole other set of serial killings. No one was ever caught for those old crimes and I got to wondering if there could be a connection."

"You found something, didn't you?"

"This afternoon, as a matter of fact." Elizabeth's excitement was contagious. "I made a breakthrough when I started looking at their genes. All the girls share one common gene."

"I don't understand. How would Ernie McDougal know something like that? He ran the bait shop."

"I don't think Ernie killed those women. Kat's mother, yes. But I think the other murders twenty years ago were done by someone else. It really clicked when you told me about Manning. Everyone knows he's a fanatic, believing that witches have powers due to a certain gene, right? He's been collecting blood samples for years now."

Brie nodded. "He wanted a sample from Nicole."

Aghast, Elizabeth stared at her. "You didn't let him have one, did you?"

"Of course not. It was all I could do to let him take one from me. Manning gives me the creeps. Are you saying he's a serial killer?"

"No. I mean, it's possible, but there's nothing to tie him to those murders. Still, I wouldn't trust him until I can be sure there is no connection between his research and this gene.''

''You don't really think his crackpot theory could be right, do you?''

''I don't know, Brie. The more I learn, the more I realize how much there is to learn. There's a strong possibility he's involved, somehow.''

''He's a respected scientist, Elizabeth!''

''I know.''

''You're starting to scare me.''

''I'm scaring me, too. After class I'm going to run these blood samples out to a friend of mine. He works for an independent laboratory about fifteen minutes from here. He agreed to test them and check my results.''

''Why not let me take them for you? I'm not about to haul Nicole and two cats over to the college tonight. As much as she adores you, I don't think my daughter will sit patiently through one of your lectures. And I know for certain the cats won't.''

''But the men want you to stay with me.''

''The weather is only going to worsen. I can run your samples out and be back before the men even know I left.''

A sudden gust of wind rattled the windows. Brie tried not to let her nervousness show.

''My mother has a bad headache tonight, Elizabeth. Dr. Thornton's coming over to see her. I need answers. Gene therapy is her only hope for a cure.''

''Manning isn't the only scientist doing this sort of research. While I'm at the college I'll talk with a couple of people and make a few calls. I know when you're scared it's easy to grab a lifeline, but let's make sure this really is a lifeline first. Okay?''

Brie nodded. She couldn't seem to stop shivering.

"Are you sure you want to run this out there for me?"

"Positive."

"All right," she agreed reluctantly. "Let me write down the directions. I have to leave in a minute to drop Brandon back at my parents' house." She glanced at the window where rain beat a steady tattoo.

"I hope Cullen and Drew will be careful."

Chapter Fourteen

He waited patiently, part of the blackness of the night. The headlights bobbed in the treetops as the car made its way up the twisty path leading to the house. He braced himself, waiting for the gate to swing open, admitting a long, dark hearse. As the vehicle drove through, he slipped inside, melding with the shadows.

His eyes were used to the night, so he had no trouble slipping unobtrusively through the tall old pines behind the hearse. When the vehicle passed inside the electrified fence surrounding the laboratory, so did he.

Wind drove the rain against his back. Since he was already wet to the skin, he ignored the sensation, but he didn't like the distant sound of thunder. Lightning posed a serious hazard here in the woods.

Manning ran inside without looking around. Unable to find another entrance or exit to the building itself, he was relieved when Manning hurried back outside, jumped back in his vehicle and drove away.

The locks proved difficult, slowing him down more than anticipated, but once inside the lab, he turned on the lights and set to work. As expected, Manning kept meticulously detailed notes, all conveniently stored on the hard drive of his computer.

Slipping a disk in the blank zip drive, he set to copying everything on the machine. One file caught his attention. Manning had been running experiments on bog people. Stunned, he took the time to scan that particular file. A member of the secret society now living in England had discovered an unexplored peat bog where, according to old church records, a number of witches had been dumped after they were hanged.

This explained a number of things. The hearse in the middle of the night. The stack of coffin-size boxes in the corner. Even the mummified body washed up on the beach a few months ago. Manning was shipping bodies into the country illegally to study.

LIGHTNING CLEAVED THE SKY. Brie gripped the wheel more tightly and dropped her speed even further. If these were merely rain bands coming in ahead of the storm, heaven help them all when the hurricane actually hit.

Wind shoved at the car, overwhelming the poor windshield wipers. Trees bent ominously, swaying over the road. But it was the lightning that really scared her. The jagged spears were blinding in their intensity. As she bypassed Old Mountain Road and the cemetery, Brie decided even a ghost wouldn't come out on a night like this. She should have gone to class with Elizabeth.

Nicole's crying was making her physically ill and she had never heard Max howl before. "Nicole, please stop crying, sweetheart. I'm trying to find a place to turn around." But the road was narrow and twisty.

"Mama, Mama, Mama!"

"Oh, baby, it's going to be okay." But Yvette's words to Drew haunted her. *"Don't let her go anywhere alone."*

Headlights came roaring out of the darkness behind her. The stupid person had his high beams on and he was driving much too fast. Too late she realized the car wasn't making any effort to slow down. The headlights filled her mirrors. Lightning and thunder came almost as one. And the car slammed into the back of hers with stunning force.

In that split second of total panic, Brie saw the tree rushing forward and knew that she was going to wreck.

DREW WATCHED THE ANGRY WAVES slap the shore, one breaker on top of another. The sky lit with heaven's fireworks, the boom of thunder barely covering the noise of the pounding surf.

The weather service should hire Brie. Her accuracy put their instruments to shame. Wet clear through, he headed to where Cullen waited in concealment. "He's not coming. We need to get back to Brie. She doesn't like storms."

"It's only been forty-five minutes." But Cullen was already moving, signaling the other two officers to call off the wait.

"What's your home number? I want to call Brie."

Drew punched the number into his cell phone. The answering machine picked up. Fear curled in his belly. "They aren't there."

"I forgot. It's Tuesday. Elizabeth is teaching a class. They must be at the college. Follow my car."

Cullen drove with reckless speed through the slippery, wet streets. Drew had all he could do to keep up with the officer. The sense that something was badly wrong hammered at him. Brie was in trouble. Drew knew it with gut-twisting intensity.

THE AIR BAG DEFLATED, filling the car with white powder. Dazed, Brie sat there. Max growled low in his throat. Turning her head, she saw his carrier had been tossed on its side. Little Imp perched on top mewing piteously. For a second, she wondered why that seemed odd. Then she remembered that Imp should be locked in her own carrier on the seat next to Nicole.

Nicole!

She tried to turn around and couldn't. The seat belt held her pinned so tightly in place it was hard to breathe.

"Nicole?"

There was no answer. Her hands fumbled for the belt's release. The metal clasp was wedged solid. Worse, the left side of her body was wedged, as well. Her left foot was trapped beneath the brake pedal somehow.

"Nicole!"

Nicole began to cry.

Relief mingled with fear. Imp jumped over the seat. Brie couldn't see her daughter. The rear view mirror was gone, a tree branch resting inside where the mirror should be. The windshield was mostly gone.

Max growled and Imp hissed as a dark shape came alongside the car and tried to open the door behind her.

Thank God someone was there to help. "Is my daughter all right? I can't move. My foot's trapped and the seat belt is jammed."

"Mama, Mama, Mama."

"It's okay, Nicole. I'm right here. Is my daughter all right?"

No one answered. The back door opened. Imp hissed loudly. There was a muffled oath and Imp yowled. Max screamed in primal rage. The sound traveled straight up her spine. Nicole began screaming as well.

"What are you doing? Let my daughter alone!"

Brie struggled against the belt's restriction, twisting to see what was happening, but all she saw was a dark shape and black-gloved hands pulling her daughter from the car, Imp clutched in her arms.

"No! Let her go! Don't take my daughter! No! Nicole—!"

THEY ARRIVED AT THE CAMPUS and Drew spotted Elizabeth's car in the parking lot immediately, but not Brie's. The storm's fury was increasing. And every light in the campus suddenly winked out, plunging the grounds into eerie darkness.

"Transformer went," Cullen said as he ran up to him. He handed Drew a flashlight. "This is going to be a hell of a night. Let's go."

POPPING THE FINAL DISK from the computer, he was startled by a thud that shook the ground. The lights winked out. The darkness of the lab was absolute. His small pocket flashlight gave him just enough light to see the computer and not much else.

It had been his intention to prowl the cold room and the main room after he finished with the files, but he'd need a much stronger light, and the files were the important thing. He couldn't allow himself to be trapped inside.

In the tomblike stillness, he heard an eerie sound, like a low moan. The hair on the back of his neck stood straight up. Wind shook the building and he relaxed. The storm, of course. Time to get out of here. His tiny beam picked up the pine boxes stacked in the corner like so many coffins.

He approached the stack and peered inside the top box. Empty. Not even packing material to indicate the contents. He started for the door when his foot hit a box off to the side. A cylinder labeled Liquid Nitrogen sat on top, and there was something different about the box underneath. He removed the tank and bent to pry off the lid when he heard someone at the door. Melting into the shadows, he waited as the door was thrown open. Wind and rain ushered in a dark-garbed figure. The light switch clicked futilely. Manning cursed and stepped back outside. He followed like a shadow.

Manning's car stood a few feet from the door. The man himself appeared in the beam of the headlights, cursing as he reached inside the car. Lifting something from the front seat, he tossed it into the bushes.

Distant lightning illuminated the area. The gate stood open. Taking advantage of the rain and darkness and Manning's preoccupation with something else inside the car, he made his way quickly to the gate as Manning carried a bundle inside. A tiny feline shape darted from the bushes, streaking toward the door.

ELIZABETH MET THE MEN OUTSIDE the main door, accompanied by a dozen students, one of whom carried a flashlight.

"Cullen! What are you doing here? Not that I'm not glad to see you. The power's out."

"Where's Brie?" Drew demanded before Cullen could respond.

"She took some samples over to Mark's lab for me."

"Alone?" Drew demanded.

"No one showed up at the wharf to meet him," Cullen said to Elizabeth grimly.

"Where's this lab?" Drew's body clamored for action. He couldn't explain the demon driving him, he only knew he had to find Brie.

Elizabeth gave him directions but added, "She should be back any minute now."

Cullen shook his head. "There's a couple of low spots along there even though the road itself climbs. She might not make it through if the road floods. Come on. We'll ride out in that direction."

"Mrs. Ryan! Mrs. Ryan!" Two young girls came running up. "Come quick! Mrs. Newman fell down the stairs."

"She isn't moving," the other girl added.

"Go," Drew told Cullen. "I'll find Brie."

"If something happens to her I'll never forgive myself," Elizabeth said.

Drew battled to keep his sports car on the road once he was out of town. Like the other side roads around Moriah's Landing this one was twisty and badly overhung with trees. Trees whose weaker branches were coming down as wind forced them to scrape the ground.

Cullen had been right about the low spots. Water sat on the road in a spreading pool outside the church and several other locations. He braked sharply as a large branch crashed to the road in front of him. As he went around it, his headlights picked up the wink of metal off to one side. Drew was out of the car and running, his mind numb with terror. A tree sprouted from the front of the little sedan. The back door gaped open. Drew heard Max yowling over the sound of the storm. He reached the driver's door. Bright red hair was spilled over the steering wheel. Brie wasn't moving. She couldn't be dead. He wouldn't let her be dead!

"Brie!"

She lifted her head. Wet from the rain whipping in through the broken windshield and open door, her face was blotchy, her eyes rimmed by tears.

"Drew! Oh, Drew, he took her! He took Nicole! I couldn't stop him. I'm trapped."

His heart thudded to a stop. Nicole's car seat was empty. So was the cat carrier beside it.

"Who took her?"

"I don't know," she sobbed.

"All right. Sit still, I'm going to get you out of here. Where are you hurt?"

"I'm not hurt. I'm stuck. My foot's trapped and the seat belt's jammed. I've tried everything, but I can't get loose. I can barely move. Drew, we've got to get her back! We've got to find Nicole!"

"We will," he vowed. Someone had taken his daughter. The enormity of that was almost paralyzing.

Drew couldn't get either of the front doors open. Pulling out his cell phone he dialed the emergency number, but the call wouldn't go through. Drew ran to the trunk. The bumper was caved in, lodging it shut. It took him a second to realize her car had been struck from behind.

All he had in his trunk was a tire iron. Desperately, he began prying at Brie's door. Headlights trapped him. He whirled, clutching the tire iron. A pickup truck coming from the opposite direction slowed to a stop. Two men about his age jumped out.

"Anyone hurt?"

Fear receded. "My wife's trapped inside."

"You're never gonna get it open that way. Let us give you a hand."

A sign on the side of the truck read D&D Construction. Between the three of them and their assortment of tools, they forced open the door and cut away the seat belt. They had to work the broken seat back until Brie could slip her foot from the twisted wreckage holding it in place.

"You okay, ma'am? You really oughta let a doctor check you over."

"Thank you. Thank you so much." She hugged each of the embarrassed men.

"Glad we could help."

"Oh, wait!" She turned unsteadily. "Where's the black box?"

"I got your purse, but I didn't see any box. You see a black box, Darrin?"

"Nope."

"It was on the floor in the back seat," she told them.

"We'll look," Drew said. "Let's get you and Max in the car out of the rain." He led her to his car and handed her the cat.

"Drew, the box contains Elizabeth's medical samples. I can't leave them. She learned something about the serial killings that might be important."

"I'll find it." But he didn't. There was no trace of the medical supplies anywhere inside or outside the car.

"Sorry, man, I don't think it's in here."

"I'm Andrew Pierce," he said, pulling a business card from his wallet. He wrote quickly on the back. "If I can ever help either of you, let me know."

"Any relation to Senator Pierce?"

"My father."

"Oh, wow. I voted for him. Hey, thanks."

"No, I thank you. Both of you."

"No problem, man. Be careful, it's nasty out here."

Drew returned to his car and turned the heater on. Brie hugged the carrier, tears running silently down her cheeks.

"Brie, are you sure you aren't hurt?"

She turned blindly toward him. "We have to get her back, Drew. We have to!"

"We will. I promise," he vowed. "Tell me exactly what happened."

Brokenly, she did. Helpless rage threatened his emotions. Where did they go to get his daughter back?

When his cell phone rang they both jumped.

"It's probably Cullen." But it wasn't.

"Does your daughter own a calico kitten?" a deep male voice asked beneath the static in his ear.

"Who is this? Where's my daughter?"

There was a long, almost puzzled pause. "Leland Manning tossed a kitten from his car a few minutes ago. He carried something into his lab."

And the phone went dead.

Because the person hung up? Or because the other person's phone cut out? There was no way to know.

"Manning has Nicole!" Brie said.

"We don't know that. This call could be another trap."

"But what if it isn't?"

Drew started the car even as he dialed the emergency number. The call still wouldn't go through. "I think the emergency line must be down."

"We have to go out there! Drew, he wanted her blood. I told him no."

"Manning wanted Nicole's blood?" And in that moment Drew understood what it meant to have his blood run cold. "What for?"

"I don't know!" Numb with fear and grief, Brie

stared at the road ahead, seeing in her mind those dark hands reaching for her child. Her daughter's screams would haunt her the rest of her life. So would every helpless minute she'd had to sit there in the dark, struggling to get free, praying for her daughter's safety. "I don't even know if Nicole was hurt in the crash," she sobbed.

Drew reached for her hand. She barely felt his touch as visions of her daughter lying dead or injured rode like a specter in her mind.

Max mewed. Brie opened the door to his carrier, seeking comfort in his soft fur while she mentally urged Drew to hurry.

"Who has access to your cell phone number?" she asked.

"It's on the answering machine in case someone really needs to reach me."

He turned onto the narrow paved lane cutting a path through the woods. Brie glimpsed a sign reading Private Road, No Trespassing. Trees hunched over the one-lane path, whipping back and forth angrily. Scattered limbs and debris forced Drew to slow almost to a crawl. They were both surprised when the twisted trees halted to create a small clearing. A tall, wrought-iron fence suddenly rose up out of the gloom. Beyond the hulking gate Brie could just make out the shape of the tall, dark spires of an estate.

"How are we going to get inside?" she asked fretfully.

"Wait here."

The headlights barely pierced the gloom. Not even a glimmer of light shone beyond their short range as rain continued to fall in blinding sheets. Brie would have welcomed the lightning back for a chance to see. She was cold, wet and frightened to her core, but all she could think about was getting her daughter back.

Drew shoved at the gate. The metal parted in eerie slow motion. Drew ran back to the car. "Brie, I think you should wait in the car."

"No."

He cupped her face. "Okay. We'll get her back together."

Brie put Max back in his carrier as they drove forward. Max protested plaintively, pawing at her through the bars. She stroked him absently with a finger as the house rose up out of the ground, an ugly, twisted, sprawling shape.

"Grab the flashlight from the glove compartment," Drew said.

Brie grabbed a screwdriver as well. It wasn't much of a weapon, but she felt better with it in her hand. Drew parked in front of the monstrosity, and together, they ran to the front door. It opened before they could knock.

A matronly woman in a long black dress held a lit taper. The tiny flame barely illuminated her stern features. "This is private property," she announced in a heavily accented voice. "You must leave."

"We're here to see Dr. Manning."

"The doctor is not here."

"Then we'll wait," Drew said, brushing past her as if she weren't trying to block his path.

"*Nein!* You cannot come in here. You must go away. Come back later!" The candle flickered madly. Distorted shadows jumped and danced against the stark white walls.

"We can't do that. I'm sorry. We don't mean to frighten you, but it is urgent we speak with Dr. Manning at once," Drew told her kindly but firmly.

"I tell you he is not here," she protested angrily.

"Where is his laboratory?" Drew asked.

"Go." A long bony finger pointed toward the front door. "You must leave here at once."

"We'll find it ourselves," Drew told her.

"*Nein!* The doctor will be upset."

Drew's expression turned so fierce even Brie was startled. "He'll be more than upset if he has our daughter."

The woman whispered something in her native tongue that could have been a prayer or a curse. Taking Brie's hand, Drew plunged into the black maw of the hall and strode toward the back of the house as if his eyes could pierce the enveloping blackness. Brie flicked on the flashlight and pressed it into his hand.

"Where are we going?"

"I'm guessing his lab is at the rear of the house. I wish I'd paid more attention when Uncle Geoffrey described it."

The house smelled of stale fried food. There was a dampness that probably came from the storm. Drew's light picked up bits of stark black-and-chrome furniture in the dark openings as they passed by rooms off the hall. When they came to a place where the hallway split, the light picked up a door at one end. They headed in that direction.

Wind caught the door, ripping it from his fingers to slam it back against the house. A low, squat building was barely visible behind the house, surrounded by a substantial fence, part of which had collapsed under the weight of a massive tree limb that had toppled onto a smaller outbuilding beside it.

"Be careful. That fence is electrified," Drew told her.

"But it looks like the tree took out the generator. We just want to make sure the current is dead."

Anticipation swelled inside her. Her daughter was here. She knew it. They ran over the muddy ground, fast turning to swampy marsh as the sodden earth struggled to absorb the continuing downpour. Drew tested the fence. Finding it dead, he led her over the broken fence and onto the grounds. A hearse sat in front of the only door she saw.

Drew detoured to the front of the vehicle and shone the flashlight on the bumper. "It's the car that hit you," he yelled, to be heard over the howl of the wind.

She grabbed his arm when he started toward the door. "Drew, wait! What if he's armed?"

"Then his first shot better count," he said savagely. "Stay behind me."

She'd never seen Drew like this. He motioned her to one side, turned the door handle and stopped. Before she could ask what he planned to do next, Drew raised his leg and kicked the lock with savage force. Once, twice, three times. On the fourth kick, the lock yielded and the metal door flew inward.

Drew stood to one side. "Manning? It's Andrew Pierce. I've come for my daughter!"

From inside came a volley of rifle shots. Drew pulled Brie down, covering her body with his own.

"Wait here!" he yelled in her ear.

"No! Drew!"

But he was already running back to the door. "Police are on their way, Manning. There's only one way out. You'd better have a lot of rounds in there. You're going to need them."

Silence met his words. Then to her horror, Drew slipped inside.

Chapter Fifteen

Heedless of the mud and water dripping off her clothes
and hair, Brie scrambled after Drew, pausing when she
reached the black maw of the open door. Her daughter
and the man she loved were inside so there wasn't any
choice. Cautiously, she inched forward.

A low, muffled moan drifted to her ears, followed by
a scraping sound. Drew? Dear God, please don't let him
be hurt. She stood still a short distance inside, straining
to hear over the howl of the wind. When the noise came
again she started forward, trying to determine the direction of the sound.

A downburst of wind sent the door slamming into the
wall. Brie jumped. Her foot kicked something that
rolled across the floor. The smell of alcohol and other
chemicals hung in the air. And the moan came once
more. Her mind replayed every horror movie she'd ever
seen. Her foot bumped against something hard and un-
yielding. Glass crunched beneath her shoe. The sounds
came from inside the box at her feet!

A powerful beam of light suddenly swept the room
from the open door at her back. Brie crouched down
beside a stack of pine boxes. Coffins!

Something pushed against the lid on the one at her

feet. A scream rose from her soul, but it never left her throat. The light from the door fastened on the coffin as the lid was thrust off. A woman's scream rolled across the room on a building wave of horror as a ghostly pale face raised its head from inside that coffin.

Brie couldn't move. The flash from a rifle muzzle and the deafening retort of the weapon came shockingly fast. She had no time to react as everything seemed to happen at once.

The scream died away as the figure in the doorway collapsed with a sickening thud. The bright beam of the flashlight rolled across the floor, tossing grotesque shadows around the strange room.

A shape lunged from between two cabinets. It slammed into the dark figure holding the rifle. And the ghostly body in front of her moaned in pain as it sat straight up in the coffin.

Brie scrambled away, hysteria bubbling in her throat. She careened into tables, cupboards and supplies, wending her way deeper into the maze without any thought save escape.

"Mama."

Amazingly, she heard the tiny whimper over the terrified pounding of her pulse.

"Nicole!"

Brie stopped moving. Objects crashed as the two figures fought. Manning and Drew?

"Mama?"

Nicole's voice sounded so weak. Confusion and the starting edge of fear laced her daughter's voice.

"Mama?"

With a resounding crash, a cabinet toppled, shattering a mix of noxious chemicals that assailed her nose.

"Mama! Mama! Mama!"

Brie ran toward her daughter's voice. A flicker of light came from behind and to her right. Barely enough to illuminate the surgical table and the tiny figure strapped beneath the looming, deadened lights.

Horrified, she rushed forward. "Hold still, sweetheart. I'm going to get you."

The light at her back grew brighter. She heard the crackle of a new danger. Fire!

Flames licked across the floor, eating the spilled alcohol in its path. Brie struggled with the straps pinning Nicole until she was free and in Brie's arms.

Smoke drifted upward with alarming speed. Drew reeled back against a lab table. Leland Manning, his face a distorted mask of rage, lifted a heavy microscope and hurled it down with smashing force against Drew's shoulder. His legs buckled. He grabbed the table for support.

"No!" Brie screamed as Manning now raised Elizabeth's black case over his head. From out of the choking cloud of smoke, the rifle spat its deadly flame. The box fell to the concrete floor and opened. Leland Manning collapsed facedown on top.

Carey Eldrich, dressed in a stained, torn tuxedo, stood there, weaving. In his hand was the rifle. He swung it toward Brie.

"Go," he said, weakly. "Get out!"

Drew was suddenly at her side, lifting his daughter from her arms. The flickering flames leaped with glee amid the dense shroud of smoke.

Carey led them to the door, staggering in obvious pain. He'd been the ghostly shape she'd seen rising inside the coffin. But there wasn't time to think about that as Drew thrust their daughter back into her arms. "Take Nicole! I'll get the housekeeper."

Only then did Brie realize it had been the house-keeper who had stood in the lab doorway with the flash-light and screamed. Drew scooped the crumpled figure from the floor as a hungry finger of flame tongued the edge of the open coffin. Carey took her elbow, making her jump. She couldn't tell if he was offering support or needing it himself, but together, they stumbled out-side with Drew at their back, holding the limp, black-garbed figure.

"Keep going!"

They moved past the hearse. A fireball exploded at their backs. Smoke spilled from the open door of the laboratory. The rasp of flames could be heard over the wind. Carey abruptly dropped to the ground. Nicole clung to Brie's neck, looking more asleep than awake.

Holding her daughter, Brie crouched beside Carey. Drew lowered the housekeeper to a patch of grass and joined her.

"Drew! Carey's hurt!"

"Can you make it to the car carrying Nicole?"

"I'll make it," she said grimly.

Pressing Nicole's face into her shoulder, she started for the downed tree and the gap in the fence where they'd originally gained entrance.

Like evil springing from the fires of hell, a flaming figure erupted from inside the burning laboratory. Le-land Manning ran straight at her, his face contorted in demonic rage.

Brie set Nicole down. She stepped in front of her and drew the screwdriver. Gripping it tightly, she stood her ground.

Cold, soulless eyes bore into her. Drew yelled, but Manning was almost on her. She braced herself, ready to thrust with the screwdriver.

A shot rang out.

Manning folded to the water-soaked ground at her feet, his clothing still burning. Brie spun, pulling Nicole against her chest to keep her daughter from seeing the grisly sight.

Drew lowered the rifle. Behind him, a dark figure pushed open the gate and sprinted across the compound. David Bryson stopped a few feet away. "I can help."

"Can you?" Drew asked coldly.

"Police and ambulance are on the way."

"How did you get through?" Brie asked nervously, moving to Drew's side. Drew slid an arm around her without taking his gaze from David Bryson. Most of David's face lay in shadow, but what Brie could see held no expression at all.

"The emergency line is back in service," he stated calmly. "Is Nicole all right?"

"I—I think so. He had her strapped to an operating table!" The remembered horror choked her.

"Let's get them out of here," David said to Drew.

Something inside the lab exploded forcefully. Brie felt the shock wave against her back.

David bent over the old woman.

"I've got Nicole. Get Carey," Brie urged Drew. He released her and squatted beside his friend.

"Come on, buddy, let's go."

Carey struggled feebly to stand. His features were drawn and pale as death.

"You...always were...a better...shot," she heard Carey whisper.

"I didn't fire the rifle," Drew responded grimly.

Their gazes went to David. His dark black jeans were tightly molded to his skin, the dark black jacket, wetly plastered against his chest. If he was armed, the weapon was well concealed.

In the confusion after the police arrived, Drew stayed behind to answer questions while Nicole and Brie were sent off in the second ambulance. Her daughter's lethargy was terrifying. Brie waited anxiously for the lab results after the doctor announced Nicole had been drugged.

When the curtain parted, she looked up, expecting Drew, but David Bryson appeared like a dark warrior. He gazed from her to her daughter, his dark eyes asking the question.

"She was drugged," Brie told him. "The doctor doesn't think it did any harm, but they're checking to see what he gave her." She'd thought she had no tears left, but one slid down her cheek all the same. "It's all my fault. I actually sought him out. I wanted Manning to help my mother. And all he wanted was Nicole for some horrible experiment."

David nodded. "Other geneticists are working with so-called 'suicide genes' to kill cancer. The therapy is viable, but Manning had a second agenda. Your daughter will be all right. I'll be in touch."

"Wait." But David slipped away.

When the curtains parted this time it was Drew. He sat on the edge of the bed beside her and stroked his daughter's cheek so tenderly it brought fresh tears to her eyes.

"The doctor got the lab report back. The drug is a common anesthetic. She's reacting exactly as she should. And odds are, she won't remember a thing. What do you say we take her home?"

He wiped her tears with the same tenderness he used on his daughter. A tiny mew came from inside the jacket he was wearing. Little Imp suddenly sprang free, jumping to the bed in a frantic effort to reach Nicole. The kitten's tiny pink tongue swiped her daughter's chin, sniffed closely, then settled itself against her sleeping daughter's chest.

"You can't bring a kitten into a hospital," Brie admonished, half laughing as she wiped at her tears.

"I won't tell if you don't."

"Where did you find her?"

"In the car inside the carrier with Max."

"That's impossible!"

Drew's face hardened. "I know."

David. She didn't know how she knew, she just did. He'd found the kitten. He'd made the call. He'd summoned help.

Or had he?

The wind didn't seem quite so fierce on the way home, but many of the roads were flooding. The cottage was dark, but it looked so normal. So safe. Drew went in first, finding the storm lanterns they kept for emergencies. Brie's eyes were gritty from too many tears, but she insisted on putting Nicole to bed herself.

Drew stroked his daughter's hand and kissed her cheek lovingly. For a moment, Brie thought her tears would start once more. But they didn't and Drew left the room. Brie put her to bed with Little Imp and Max looking on. Imp immediately jumped up to curl on the pillow beside Nicole. Brie kissed her daughter's forehead before going in search of Drew.

He stood at the window gazing broodingly out at the night. Like Brie, he was still wearing the wet clothing he'd had on all evening.

"You should change," she said softly.

He turned. "So should you."

She let that slide. "Why did Manning want Nicole?"

"No doubt he wanted her blood," Drew said bitterly, "just like he told you."

"That doesn't make sense. He didn't have to kidnap her and strap her to an operating table."

She realized Drew's anger at what had been done to their daughter matched her own.

"You know his pet theory about witches and special powers?" Drew began to pace before the gas fireplace. "According to my mother, our family is also descended from one of the most powerful witches who ever lived in Moriah's Landing."

Brie stared at him in shock.

Drew stopped, shrugged. "I just got off the cell phone with her. Manning must have thought he'd found the perfect subject for his crackpot theory."

"Nicole's just a little girl!"

"Carey told Cullen Ryan that Manning had been injecting him with something since he was kidnapped. He was using Carey to test out his theory. Manning claimed it was only justice since it was Carey's fault he'd had to kill his wife—"

"Leland Manning killed Ursula? But I thought she was kidnapped!"

"Cullen never was too happy with that story."

"But the money—"

"We think he withdrew it to pay for the bodies he was having shipped into the country illegally."

"What bodies?"

"This all ties in with the investigation Jonah Reis was doing for the FBI. Jonah knew someone in the secret society was smuggling something into the country from overseas. When he and Kat were investigating, they discovered coffins filled with bodies. Jonah and

Cullen deduced Manning was smuggling the bodies to use in his research.''

''He wouldn't need entire bodies to do genetic research.''

''Normally, you're right, but these were reputed witches from England who lived in the 1500s. I imagine the chance to examine them was irresistible.''

Brie gaped, wondering when this nightmare would end.

''Jonah thinks a member of the secret society now living in England found an unknown peat bog where witches were dumped after they were killed.''

She shook her head, too bewildered to even question such insanity.

''Actually, I've heard of this. Scientists have found perfectly preserved bodies dating back to the 1500s in peat bogs. Fortunately, it's Jonah and Cullen's problem. Cullen knew Ursula Manning was killed by a rifle shot from the woods and he suspected Manning all along.''

''So Manning kidnapped Carey because of the affair he had with Ursula?''

''Looks that way. The attacks on me stopped right after Carey admitted his involvement with Ursula. She was supposed to meet him in the woods that morning, but she never showed up. She told Carey that Manning only married her because her ancestors dated back to the Salem witch trials.''

''Then why didn't Manning try to kill Carey like he tried to kill you when he thought you were the one having an affair with his wife?''

''Manning told Carey he planned to open Carey's brain and inject a gene he had isolated to see if it would reproduce and cause Carey to develop some sort of psychic talent or something.''

"That's crazy!"

Drew nodded. "As Carey put it, Manning gives new life to the Hollywood image of a mad scientist. The worst part is, the court system will probably find him mentally incompetent to stand trial for his crimes."

Horrified, Brie stared at Drew. "He's still alive?"

"I'm afraid so. He's badly burned, but the bullet didn't hit any vital organs. The doctors expect him to pull through."

Brie shuddered. "What about Carey?"

"He has a concussion, cuts and bruises, he's dehydrated, and weaker than Little Imp from being drugged and locked up in that coffin. And while I don't imagine he's going to be fond of enclosed places anymore, he's going to be fine."

"Thank God. We should have stopped to see him before we left the hospital."

Drew shook his head. "He wouldn't have appreciated our company. Nancy was there."

"So there is something going on between the two of them."

"Looks that way. What about us?"

The world seemed to stop. "What?"

Drew walked over to stand directly in front of her. "Why do you think I married you?"

"Is this a trick question?"

"No. Just give me an honest answer."

Her heart began pounding irrationally. "We both know why you married me," she said sadly.

"Do we?"

"Of course. You needed to save your career and you wanted to be part of Nicole's life."

"And you married me to pay for your mother's experimental treatment," he said bleakly. "So my uncle was right when he called our marriage a sham. A marriage of convenience.''

''I don't understand. Why do you look so angry?''

''Maybe because I'm not finding this marriage one bit convenient,'' he snapped.

His words were like tiny razors, flaying her heart.

''I don't want a sham of a marriage,'' he announced.

Her own anger, usually carefully controlled, sprang to life. ''Well what *do* you want?'' she demanded.

He grabbed her shoulders. ''You. Loving me.''

The silence was deafening. ''What?'' she whispered.

He let her go and strode over to where Max sat perched on the arm of a chair watching them. Stroking the cat gently, he went on more quietly.

''Do you know what my mother told me tonight? Manning might actually have been on to something about witches and their genes. She informed me that my staid, huffy, highly educated father actually believes that stuff. He thinks I have an unnatural ability. Charm. Don't you love it? He thinks my mother's incredible green thumb is as unnatural as my supposed ability to charm everyone I meet. Everyone except my own wife, of course.''

''Are you saying you want to charm me?'' Brie reeled from the implication of his words. Was it possible? Did Drew want what she wanted?

Drew snorted. He turned back to the window. ''The storm's finally moving off. We were lucky. The hurricane moved up the coast, but never actually made landfall. All this damage was nothing more than a passing blow.''

Just like Drew's words.

''When I saw your wrecked car tonight,'' he continued, "I knew if you were dead, part of me was going to die right there, too. Sounds sappy, doesn't it?"

She shook her head, but he didn't turn around, so he didn't see the hope blossoming inside her.

"I have to tell you, Brie, I have never been so scared as I was tonight when Manning came at you and you just stood there protecting Nicole, holding that ridiculous screwdriver like some street fighter with a knife. I grabbed the rifle, but I knew I was going to be too late. You were going to die and I wanted to die, too."

He turned around and she saw the moisture in his eyes.

"I love you, Brie. I've loved you since that stupid party four years ago. I think I knew it even then, but I was young and stupid and— I don't want a sham of a marriage, Brie, I—"

She launched herself into his arms, laughing, crying, her heart filled to bursting. "I love you, I love you, I love you."

He grabbed her, giving her a shake.

"You love me?"

"Since I was ten years old and Tasha took a group of us to watch your baseball game. Josie Farleigh knocked my drink over to be mean. You saw her do it and you bought me a drink *and* a candy bar."

"Why don't I remember that?"

"Because I was ten and you were sixteen and there was a girl with long blond hair you were trying to impress."

"Ridiculous." But a smile edged his lips. His intense blue eyes were practically glowing. "I don't even like blondes. I prefer redheads."

"Really?"

"I'll prove it. What do you say we go and check out the bedroom?"

"Oh, God, I love you so much, Drew."

He pulled her tightly against his chest. She felt the certainty and the power of his words when he spoke against her ear.

"I love you, too, Brie."

Kissing her with incredible tenderness, he slid his arm around her waist and reached for the light switch. At least for the moment, the ghosts of Moriah's Landing were at peace.

And the story continues....
Next month don't miss
the last installment of
MORIAH'S LANDING:
BEHIND THE VEIL
by Joanna Wayne

Chapter One

David Bryson walked the rocky path along the edge of the craggy cliffs and stared down at the swirling water as it crashed against the treacherous rocks below. Once the sight had filled him with awe and excitement. Now it was only a bitter reminder that it was the place where he had lost his world.

Some claimed he'd also lost his sanity that horrible night five years ago, and perhaps they were the ones who understood best.

Instinctively, his hand moved to his face, and his fingers traced the jagged lines of the scar that ran from his right temple to below his ear. The scar on his face, his conspicuous limp and the hideous patches of coarse, red skin on his chest and stomach were always with him to remind him of the explosion.

Still, the plastic surgeons had worked wonders, rebuilt his face, transformed him from something so ghastly he couldn't step into public without a mask. The doctors had saved his life even while he'd begged them for the release of death. To this day, he had never fully forgiven them.

"Dr. Bryson."

He turned at the sound of his name and located the

lone figure standing behind the Bluffs. The man was no more than an outline in the deepening darkness, but David didn't have to see his butler to recognize him. He knew the voice well.

He waved and called up to him. "I'm down here, Richard."

David took one last look at the water below him, then tilted his face and examined the turbulent layers of dark clouds before starting back up the rocky path.

Too bad about the gathering storm, but if the carnies were lucky, it would hold off for a few hours. The carnival had been a highlight of the fall season for years, coming to town just after the students at the all-girls college of Heathrow had plunged into the sea of sorority activities and before they became immersed in serious studies.

Memories sneaked into his mind. A kiss at the top of the Ferris wheel, Tasha's body pressing into his as they spun on the Tilt-a-Whirl.

A ragged ache tore at his insides. He fought it by pushing his body to its limits, ignoring the stabbing pain in his right leg and jogging up the slippery path that ran along the edge of the cliff. In minutes, he'd covered the ground between him and Richard and stopped at the man's side.

"You risk your life when you do that, sir."

"What do you expect from a madman?"

"Indeed. You're no more mad than I am."

"You need to get out more, Richard. Mingle with the townspeople. They'll tell you what an insane monster you work for."

"I take no stock in the tales of people who walk around in fear that some old ghost is going to rise from the cemetery and kill their virgins."

"Ghost tales are good for tourism."

"They're the invention of superstitious fools. There's evil in this town, cruelty, too. But it doesn't come from ghosts or witches." Richard turned and started back toward the house. David followed him, wondering as always what he'd do without the man.

Richard Crawford had come to work for him five and a half years ago when David had returned to Moriah's Landing and purchased the Bluffs. Richard's hair had grayed around the ears since then and receded from his forehead, but he was still fit and youthful for a man who'd celebrate his sixtieth birthday this year.

More important, Richard was probably the only one who understood how much David still loved his dead fiancée. He missed Tasha's voice, her smile, the way she'd made him feel. She'd been so young and innocent. And beautiful.

"Will you be going out tonight, sir?"

"Maybe later. First I plan to go back to the lab and work."

The question was ritual. The answer was automatic. After dinner, he routinely went back to the test tubes and microscopes that filled the west wing of the Bluffs. He'd work until his mind was numb and fatigue robbed him of the control that kept his inner demons in check. Then he'd lose all perspective and turn into the madman everyone believed him to be.

He'd slip from the confines of his lonely castle and drive to the edge of town. He'd park his car and walk the streets and back alleys, searching endlessly for answers he never found. One day he would. And when he did, revenge would be swift and unbelievably sweet.

Becca Smith was not part of the answers or the revenge. But lately, he'd ended up on her street far too often. Something about her haunted him, and try as he might, he couldn't seem to shake her from his mind.

Richard paused at the back door. "I hear the whole town is gearing up for the Fall Extravaganza. Perhaps you should go. One night of fun won't ruin your reputation as a serious scientist."

He touched his fingers to the scar. "I'd frighten the children."

"With one little scar? I seriously doubt that, sir."

"With one *ghastly* scar. I suppose I could dig out the mask I wore in the first years after the explosion and go as the Phantom."

"Just go as yourself. I predict you'll be pleasantly surprised."

David turned away. "Moriah's Landing has always had lots of surprises for me. Only one was ever pleasant, and in the end, it was the cruelest surprise of all."

"That was five years ago. Besides, test tubes make lonely bedfellows."

"True, but they never pull away in disgust when I stand in front of them."

David pushed through the door and stepped inside the bleak interior of the Bluffs. Nothing but grays and browns and thick, opaque draperies. Tasha had planned to redecorate the place, fill it with light and brighter fabrics to complement the richness of the dark woods of the furniture.

Her plans had died with her. Without Tasha, there was no light. Besides, he'd lost all interest in the structure that had so intrigued him when he'd purchased it. Now he spent most of his days in the lab or out staring at the water breaking over the treacherous rocks at the foot of the jagged cliffs.

A bleak and isolated life. But a few miles away, the

carnival was in full swing. Coeds' laughter, painted horses, music, a kaleidoscope of colors. And for the first time in five long years, he felt himself *almost* wishing he were part of it.

He closed his eyes for a second as Richard walked ahead of him toward the kitchen. He expected Tasha's face to materialize in his mind, but this time it was the image of Becca Smith that danced behind his eyelids. Tall and willowy, her long blond hair falling around her shoulders.

He'd have to be very careful if he left the house tonight. And he knew he'd leave. The town was already beckoning.

A ROYAL MONARCH'S SEARCH FOR AN HEIR LEADS TO DANGER IN:

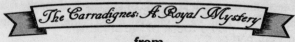

The Carradignes: A Royal Mystery

from
HARLEQUIN®
INTRIGUE®

Plain-Jane royal secretary Ellie Standish wanted one night to shine. But when she was mistaken for a princess and kidnapped by masked henchmen, this dressed-up Cinderella had only one man to turn to—one of her captors: a dispossessed duke who had his own agenda to protect her and who ignited a fire in her soul. Could Ellie trust this man with her life...and her heart?

Don't miss:
THE DUKE'S COVERT MISSION
JULIE MILLER June 2002

And check out these other titles in the series

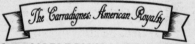

The Carradignes: American Royalty

available from HARLEQUIN AMERICAN ROMANCE:

THE IMPROPERLY PREGNANT PRINCESS
JACQUELINE DIAMOND March 2002

THE UNLAWFULLY WEDDED PRINCESS
KARA LENNOX April 2002

THE SIMPLY SCANDALOUS PRINCESS
MICHELE DUNAWAY May 2002

And coming in November 2002:
THE INCONVENIENTLY ENGAGED PRINCE
MINDY NEFF

Available at your favorite retail outlet.

HARLEQUIN®
Makes any time special ®

Visit us at www.eHarlequin.com

HICR

Nail-biting mystery…
Sensuous passion…
Heart-racing excitement…
And a touch of the unknown!

Silhouette®
DREAMSCAPES…

four captivating paranormal romances promising all
of this—and more!

Take a walk on
the dark side with:

THE PIRATE AND
HIS LADY
by Margaret St. George

TWIST OF FATE
by Linda Randall Wisdom

THE RAVEN MASTER
by Diana Whitney

BURNING TIMES
by Evelyn Vaughn
Book 2 of The Circle

*Coming to a store near you
in June 2002.*

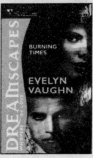

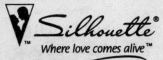

Silhouette®

Where love comes alive™

Visit Silhouette at www.eHarlequin.com   RCDREAM7

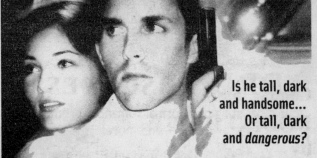

TRUEBLOOD, TEXAS

Coming in May 2002...

RODEO DADDY
by

B.J. Daniels

Lost:
Her first and only love.
Chelsea Jensen discovers
ten years later that her father
had been to blame for
Jack Shane's disappearance
from her family's ranch.

Found:
A canceled check. Now Chelsea
knows why Jack left her. Had he ever loved her, or had she
been too young and too blind to see the truth?

Chelsea is determined to track Jack down and find out.
And what a surprise she gets when she finds him!

Finders Keepers: bringing families together

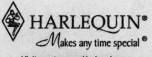